PROMETHEUS WAKES

PROMETHEUS WAKES

THE GREAT INSURRECTION™ BOOK FOUR

DAVID BEERS

MICHAEL ANDERLE

DISRUPTIVE IMAGINATION

Copyright © 2021 LMBPN Publishing
Cover Art by Jake @ J Caleb Design
http://jcalebdesign.com / jcalebdesign@gmail.com
Cover copyright © LMBPN Publishing
A Michael Anderle Production

LMBPN Publishing
PMB 196, 2540 South Maryland Pkwy
Las Vegas, NV 89109

Version 1.00, 2021
eBook ISBN: 978-1-64971-608-8
Print ISBN: 978-1-64971-609-5

THE PROMETHEUS WAKES TEAM

Thanks to our Beta Readers

Kelly O'Donnell, John Ashmore, Rachel Beckford

Thanks to our JIT Readers

Dave Hicks
Diane L. Smith
Jackey Hankard-Brodie
Angel LaVey

Editor

SkyHunter Editing Team

DEDICATION

For my brother, Danny.

— David

*To Family, Friends and
Those Who Love
to Read.
May We All Enjoy Grace
to Live the Life We Are
Called.*

— Michael

THE WRITTEN HISTORY OF THE GREAT INSURRECTION

We found ourselves with a powerful group of soldiers, a leader who seemed to have no limits, and a mission that everyone was willing to die for.

We had, through luck and courage, beaten back an imperial regime. They'd chased us to the edges of the universe and sent their best after us, and we had defeated them. Their dreadnoughts were returning to Earth, and while we knew they weren't done with us, we had time.

Any outside observer would think we were in a good position.

The truth was far different.

We were closer to death than we had ever imagined. We just didn't know it.

CHAPTER ONE

The Myrmidon Ajax had known the AllMother would return to her people. She might leave for a time, but she could never leave forever. Ajax had decided to wait for her.

While the AllMother and her Prophesied One rushed across the universe to save someone who was little more than an insect in the overall plan, Ajax went to the planet Phoenix.

The fire that raged in their atmosphere did nothing to the Myrmidon ships. The flames might as well have not been there.

The Terram were not a stupid people. When Ajax landed, they didn't offer any resistance. While they had remained out of the AllSeer's path for much of their history, they knew about the Myrmidons. They knew that neighboring planets bent the proverbial knee when Myrmidons arrived, so they did the same.

There was no battle. No death. Just the knowledge that as long as they obeyed the Myrmidons' wishes, things could go back to normal when they left.

Ajax hadn't asked for elaborate quarters, although he didn't think these small men had any. Indeed, the Myrmidons were entirely too large to walk through these rock-carved halls for long.

Inside the tiny room Ajax had been given, he called on the AllSeer.

"I am here, my lord," he said from his knees. His head was bowed, so he didn't see the dark shadow standing next to the far wall. "Do you wish her people to live, or would you have me kill them?"

The refugees who had fled Pluto remained on Phoenix, waiting for their supposed saviors to return. Ajax could run through them quickly, and when the AllMother returned, only death would greet her. Ajax had no preference in the matter.

The shadow remained quiet for a few moments before saying, "You have done well, Ajax. Do not hurt her people. We have no quarrel with them. To kill them would only inspire hatred from my sister, and it would not help our cause. Regardless of what she thinks, our fate is not to destroy the universe but to help it reach its destiny."

"Yes, my lord. It will be done." Ajax looked up at the shadow. "What about her Prophesied One?"

"If he will bend the knee, we shall welcome him. Not as a Superior, but not as a slave, either. He will be under us, but above our slaves."

"If he doesn't bend?" Ajax asked.

"Kill him."

Alexander de Finita sat on his throne, staring out into space. His Praetorian Guard stood at the edges of the circular room. For the first time in his life, Alexander was at a loss to understand what had happened.

His two Primuses had deserted the Commonwealth. In the government's entire history, nothing like that had ever happened.

From all reports, Hel vi Thraxus was dead. The Commonwealth spies said that rumor was Ares himself killed her before helping free the man he'd been sent to kill.

Alexander had not yet talked to the Fathers. He had no desire to do so, yet sooner or later, he would have to go to that orb and hear his chastisement. Alexander was starting to think they might be right, and he was a fool for doubting them. Had he overestimated his strength? The Commonwealth's? It seemed almost impossible for Alistair Kane to do what he'd done, yet here they were.

The comm on his throne's armrest lit up with a small purple light. Alexander knew who was outside the room since he'd summoned the man. Perhaps he should have summoned him earlier. Alexander didn't know anymore. All he truly knew was that he'd been too lax in all areas of his rule. They should have ended this former Titan on Pluto, but his godsdamned Primus had been too cowardly to do what was needed *when* it was needed. She'd hesitated, and Kane had escaped.

Alexander shook his head in disgust.

He tapped the purple button. "Let him in."

The massive double doors opened, and a man slightly older than the Ascendant stepped inside. He was plainly dressed in a brown garment that covered his entire body. His hair was long, to his shoulders, and gray. His beard was close-cropped and gray as well. He looked like a man who cared about his appearance but not because of what others might think. His dress was meticulous if simple because that was how he wanted to present himself.

The man walked toward the throne, taking a knee at the appropriate place. "You summoned me, my liege?"

"Thank you for coming. I know it's a long trip." The man had come from Mars, which he'd retired to more than two decades ago.

"As long as I breathe, I will serve the Commonwealth, my liege."

The man's name was Caius de Gracilis, and he was not someone to be trifled with. The Ascendant knew that, and he also knew he needed this man. He'd gone to Hel first, thinking an assassin could handle this issue. That was no longer the case.

"I am certain you're aware of what happened to Pluto?" Alexander asked.

"Yes. A regrettable if necessary action to eliminate the Subversives."

Oh, the old man played the game as well as anyone who'd ever lived. Alexander stood up. "Please rise, Caius. Will you walk with me?"

"Of course, my liege." The old man stood quickly, like someone half his age.

Alexander stepped off his throne and walked to the old man. He offered his arm and the other took it, both grabbing the lower arm of the other. "It's good to see you again," the Ascendant said in a less formal manner.

"Likewise, my liege."

Alexander led the Martian outside the throne room and toward the upper portion of the Imperial Residence. They remained quiet until they reached the transport. "Have you been to the clouds?" Alexander asked.

"No, my liege. I've never had the opportunity."

"Come. I think you'll enjoy it," the Ascendant responded.

The two got into the transport, followed by a single Praetorian Guard, and flew high above the world. It finally stopped in the middle of a white cloud. The side door opened, sliding into the wall, but no wind rushed in. The transport had latched onto a walkway, one that had been built two generations ago. Alexander's grandfather had enjoyed long walks, but he wanted to be alone when he did it, so he'd built this track among the clouds. It floated above the family's domicile and was protected by a laser defense system.

They were untouchable here, but the Praetorian followed at a short distance.

"You know it's all bullshit, don't you?" Alexander asked as they began their walk.

Caius looked down at the transparent floor. The clouds moved beneath him, and where they thinned, the world below was visible. "I figured as much. If we could destroy the Subversive movement by burning Pluto, we would have done it during Aurelius' time."

He was referring to Alexander's ancestor—the first Imperial Ascendant, the man who'd started this mess and one of the Fathers who sat in that globe dictating to him what should happen. *He* was the one who'd made all of it possible.

Caius said nothing else but waited for Alexander to speak. He was a smart man and wouldn't be rushed into mistakes.

"How is Mars treating you?" the Ascendant asked.

"It is at your disposal, as always, my liege."

"The truth, Caius. It's only us here."

The old man grinned and looked over his shoulder at the guard. The point was made. The Ascendant was never alone. He stopped walking and looked above him. White clouds passed slowly around them. "Ruling a planet is a pain in the ass, Alexander, if it's the truth you demand." He brought his head back down and began walking again. "Though ruling a star system is probably more of one, so I'm sure you understand."

"That I do, Caius."

The old man was one of the very few people who had been able to transcend his family's lineage. He had been born to an upper house, become a ferocious Titan, a Primus in his own right, and then retired early to become Mars' Imperial Propraetor. There he ruled subject only to the Imperial Ascendant, and the man had done a fine job by any measurement.

"The Commonwealth is in trouble, Caius, and I don't think either of us has the time to act like we don't know what's going on. I know you have birds that whisper to you, just as I do. You're aware of the former Titan we've been trying to kill?"

Caius nodded. He placed his hands behind his back as

they came to a bend in the track. "He's the one they say was better than me, right?"

The Ascendant shrugged. "Some, yes. Who can know, given the age difference?"

"Yes, I'm aware of...some happenings," the old man said. Alexander knew what he meant; that the propraetor knew about everything that'd happened. From Hel to that snot-nosed brat Ares deserting the Commonwealth, he was aware.

Are you thinking this might be your time to rise, old man? Perhaps you or your son could rule better than me?

Alexander showed nothing of his thoughts. "I'm no longer going to chase him around the universe. We will have our spies watching him, but the concern now is that he's going to return, and when he does, he'll have an army at his disposal. Some think this might even be the Commonwealth's end."

He said the words without explaining who the some were. A man such as Caius wouldn't need it spelled out. He had never seen the orb or heard the Fathers speak, but he knew of it.

"What would you have me do, my liege?" The lightness in his voice disappeared as the situation's gravity became apparent.

"We have perhaps six months to ready ourselves. I will need you to marshal the other propraetors and all their strength from the seven planets. Both the Sanctum and the Edge. We'll need it all to repel this."

Caius took a few more steps without speaking. "It's not just him, is it?"

Alexander shook his head. "No."

"It's true then?" Caius asked. "The twins are returning?"

Alexander nodded. "We've been able to retrieve some of the Primuses' holovids. Their personal ones. They didn't know a lot, but what they did hear was the same thing we were told when we were next in line. The brother and sister see this as some kind of cosmic struggle. The woman thinks this former Titan will lead them out of the wilderness. The male twin? Who knows what he thinks, but he's chased her to the ends of the universe. He'll chase her here, too."

Alexander was speaking more than he should, but the old man had a disarming way about him. Every propraetor wanted to be the Imperial Ascendant. It had been a birthright since the beginning, but only because of the strength the de Finitas held and the AI system calculating every possible move someone might make. Still, if the propraetors saw blood in the water, they'd swarm.

Strength must hold, and Caius had to know that.

"We can defeat them. I'm not worried about that. The Commonwealth is simply too strong to lose, but we must come together as one. You understand, Caius?"

"Of course, my liege."

They walked another large portion of the track in silence, then Caius spoke again. His voice wasn't that of someone playing a game but of someone trying to understand the truth of the matter. "This is it, isn't it? The Commonwealth can rule for another thousand years or fall in the next six months. Is that about it?"

"Yes," Alexander answered.

Caius de Gracilis went to the room assigned to him.

He was sixty-two years old and thought the current Imperial Ascendant an arrogant, cruel man. Caius understood the cruelty. Anyone at that height of power had to have a streak of cruelty to keep said power. It was the arrogance Caius could never understand. They'd been given this life, and that was something Caius never forgot. True, they had to continually earn what they'd been given, but in the beginning, this royalty was handed to them.

He met with de Finita once a year, the same as all the propraetors. You didn't want to meet with him more often; it meant there was something wrong with your propraetorship. When Caius had been summoned to Earth, he'd thought one of two things were happening. Either he would be assassinated to make way for some upstart to take over Mars—although this would cause a war with his family, but the Ascendant would win it.

Or he was being summoned for this very reason: the Commonwealth was in danger.

Could it be so? Caius had seen this former Titan once a long time ago, ten or fifteen years after his own retirement. The man had been a perfect specimen. He looked like something created to arouse women, and from what Caius had been told, his battle skills were unrivaled. So those people who saw him said, although they'd quickly forgotten what Caius had been capable of.

Caius understood the problems with the Commonwealth. He understood that he was a large part of those problems, a ruler who refused to give up his seat and would pass it down to his son. Yet, he knew the good the Commonwealth did too. He was versed in his history and understood the sheer terror that mankind had brought on itself and the environment before the One People, One Purpose mantra took hold. The Commonwealth had conquered a star system and allowed humanity to venture to the farthest reaches of the universe.

There might be problems with it, but that didn't mean you threw it all away. The good far outweighed the bad, and Caius had served the Commonwealth for far too long to not see that.

Caius sat in one of the room's chairs. It was much too soft for his liking, like everything on Earth. Other planets were soft in their nature, too, but not Mars. The red planet was hard. It was hard to rule, and that came from the hard living of its inhabitants. Earth had been cowed long ago, then had given the best of everything to pacify the masses. In truth, the Earthborn were probably not ready for a war of this magnitude. They weren't hard enough.

Caius pulled up a DataTrack and began looking into the former Titan. He knew all about the old woman and the old man, the twins who would soon be returning. He didn't know enough about this warrior, though.

He read until the night was late or the morning early.

He asked his network what they knew about the happenings in the other galaxy. He always kept his ears alert to whispers of major events, but now he dove deep, wanting to understand at a granular level.

When he was finished, Caius didn't know if it was luck, the gods, or talent that had kept Kane alive. A mixture of all three, perhaps. Caius understood that the gods did not listen to prayers but that sometimes they would intervene in the universe's affairs. Maybe this was one of those rare times. The man certainly had talent.

When he read about Kane's wife, he thought he finally understood. The Ascendant did too, which was why he'd brought the woman to the Imperial Residence.

A love-stricken man, who would sacrifice society for that love.

Alistair Kane had no honor. He was a foolish young man in Caius' eyes, talented or not. Someone who would destroy the greatest civilization ever known to get a woman back? He could hardly be considered a man; he was more like a child. This was a child's errand after all.

Love...

Love was a fairy tale. Did family matter? Of course, but the greater good of society mattered more than any one man's wishes.

Caius sighed. He knew he was too old to face this man down. The best of the Commonwealth had failed. Caius understood his responsibility. It was the same as it had always been: to protect the Commonwealth. He would need to speak to the other propraetors. They would have to be together on this.

The foolish man and his army would be stopped.

The Ascendant was an arrogant man but intelligent. He knew Caius' honor would force him to do what was necessary. He would marshal the others, and the full force of the Commonwealth would come to bear on this child.

CHAPTER TWO

Alistair had not rushed back to the planet Phoenix. After Ares left, Alistair went back into his reclusive state. He didn't go to Thoreaux or the AllMother again. Servia brought him the information he needed. Obs mostly stayed at his side, though he sometimes wandered around the fortress.

For the first time in his life, Alistair truly felt lost. He no longer understood who he was. He didn't understand what he'd been able to do, and sitting in his room alone, he couldn't replicate it. He couldn't move anything. He couldn't read minds. He couldn't tell when Servia was outside his door. He'd done something that should be impossible, and he couldn't do it again.

He didn't know himself anymore. The physical change had been one thing, but this was something else entirely.

After another week, he realized he couldn't figure this out by himself. He couldn't figure it out with another person, either. He didn't know how much he could trust the AllMother any longer. In order to understand who—or what—he was, he'd have to go back out into the world. He could sit in this room and sulk forever if he wanted. Manius had made that clear. He was a valuable asset to the underworld king, an asset that now controlled an entire army of gigantes and was himself a force of nature.

Alistair hadn't undergone this change to sit here and think, though.

The purpose was still the same. Perhaps enlarged, but the core? Luna. The overthrow of the Commonwealth. Whatever it took so that he and his wife could be together again.

So, the god-like creature told his council that they were returning to Phoenix. They scheduled a private shuttle, one that could handle his new army, and they set sail.

A few weeks passed, but finally, Alistair could see the burning planet again. It wasn't quite like a star, but close. The atmosphere contained the roiling heat, but one could see it burning from a long way away.

They were a day from landing when the AllMother came to Alistair's room. She knocked lightly on the door.

Obs perked his ears up but left his head on the floor.

"Come in," Alistair called. He was lying on his cot with a DataTrack, reading.

He glanced at the door as she entered, then turned his eyes back to the words projected above his eyes.

"I'm sorry to interrupt," the old woman said, "but we need to talk."

Alistair flicked his eyes in her direction. "What is it?"

"The Myrmidons. They've taken over Phoenix. They're waiting for me."

Alistair put the DataTrack down and sat up. Obs

pushed himself up as well, both now looking at the AllMother. "What do you mean? The shuttle has been in contact with Phoenix daily. They've mentioned nothing." Even as he spoke the words, he understood how naive they were. If the Myrmidons were on Phoenix, the Terram were certainly under their control. They wouldn't be able to say anything.

The AllMother must have seen the realization on his face. She nodded. "I feel them now. My abilities are weakening, yes, but they're waiting for me. I'm certain of it."

Alistair leaned forward and placed his elbows on his knees. "Any idea how many there are?"

"No. I can't see that."

Alistair didn't think of asking her what to do. That part of his life had passed when he nearly blew up a stadium with his mind. He understood now that whatever happened with this group of people was down to him, and only him. If the AllMother had advice, she could speak up. He wasn't going to sacrifice her to the Myrmidons, obviously, but...

He looked up. "Why does he want you?"

The AllMother gave a knowing smile. "You cut to the core of the matter quickly, Prometheus. I've never told anyone what it is between us. Would you like to hear now? Do you think it'll help you make your decision?"

"I think I have to. I need to know everything. There can't be any more secrets between us."

The old woman sighed and looked at her shoes. "Perhaps you're right. Do you mind if I sit down?"

He motioned to the chair that sat under the desk. She moved to it, and Obs sat just in front of Alistair's legs. The drathe laid down and faced the AllMother as she pulled the chair out and sat down.

"There are a few stages to this, Pro," she told him. "I'm going to tell it all to you. It's the only way you'll understand and can make the right decision."

He flipped back onto the cot and laid down, then placed his hands on his chest and interlaced his fingers. "Tell me."

CHAPTER THREE

Alex had just left her father down in the lab where he'd had her operated on. He'd had her modified. She stalked up from the medbay with red irises. She'd discarded a troop of Praetorian Guards with a thought, and she knew others would be looking for her. She didn't care. Alex didn't understand what had happened to her, or the extent of what she could do, but she did know that hurting her would be a difficult thing to accomplish.

She reached the first floor of the family's home and stood in the foyer. It stretched for many yards in each direction, and she saw more Praetorians on the other side. They stopped walking as they saw her standing in her gown, somehow different than the woman who had been led down to the medbay.

"If you come for me, you will die," she called across the foyer.

The lead Praetorian must have taken it as a challenge, though no one would ever know. He'd taken his second step toward her, and Alex reached out with her mind. His head turned three-hundred-and-sixty degrees before he took his third step.

The man hit the ground, the impact of his gear echoing loudly off the high ceilings.

The other Praetorians didn't move, only stared at this being who none of them understood. She'd become something written about in horror and science fiction novels for hundreds of years. In their eyes, she was no longer human but something other.

"When I am gone," she called again, "my father will need medical attention. He's in the medbay. Someone relay the message that if he comes for me, he'll die as your leader just did."

Alex whisked to the left and made her way to her quarters, the ones she'd had before she'd been locked up for a month. She found her clothing still there, and she changed from the medbay gown to pants and a shirt. She pulled boots on, not knowing where she was going but realizing her shoes would need to be ready for anything.

Once she'd finished dressing, she headed to the second medbay on the premises. She knew how her father thought. He would want brother and sister to be separated at all costs. Uniting them could lead to a diminishment of his power.

People were rushing around the premises, and she knew why. There were dead people lying about, and the servants would be panicking. When they saw her with red eyes, she saw the fear in them.

The second medbay was empty of personnel when she arrived. The doctors must have panicked when they heard about what had happened with Alex. They weren't going to risk seeing her brother act the same way. The layout was nearly identical, though, and lying inside two tubes were two different versions of her twin brother.

Alexander, named after the most famous Alexander of all time.

Neither of them was awake, so something had gone wrong. They had awakened, but it hadn't been time. Alex had thought *her physical body would be changed, but she came to with some-thing very different inside her mind. What would her brother be like?*

She walked over to the glass tube the first figure lay in. She raised her hand to touch it, but paused as she saw what was inside.

There was no question about what had changed with her brother.

Alexander had always been a perfect physical specimen. Strong and muscular, his athletic skills had been superior throughout his life.

What Alex saw now was something else. Her brother had been big but not beast-like. The creature lying in the tube was larger than any human had a right to be. Muscle rippled along his bare legs, and the flesh of his shoulders looked like it might split the skin holding it in. Veins wove their way across his arms, torso, and legs.

Alexander was taller by a few feet, too. Even his facial struc-ture had changed. The bones were thicker, his forehead and jawline jutting out farther. He still held the classic beauty he'd been born with, but now there was a rawness to it, a danger.

Alex's red eyes grew wet. They had destroyed her brother. They'd turned him into some kind of monstrosity.

And what did they do to you? *her psyche asked.* The only difference is your monster can't be seen with the eye.

She had to get him out of here. Regardless of his flaws and faults as a human, he didn't deserve this.

Alex looked at the farthest glass container. She didn't even know which one was her brother and which was the clone. Gods, she didn't even know which one she was. She did the only thing she could think of at the moment; she went to the same container she'd been in, the one closest to the door. At the bottom was a panel. Alex had studied medicine, as had Alexander. She understood the basics of what she now saw. A de Finita was expected to be knowledgeable on almost any subject, and Alex had taken that responsibility seriously. She understood what she was reading. Her brother's transformation was done, and he was under anesthesia right now to keep him unconscious.

Alex pressed buttons on the panel, and gas slowly started seeping into the tube from the bottom. Her brother's chest moved up and down, taking in the gas that would wake him.

Alex checked the door of the medbay. No one had arrived. She had no doubt they were coming. Something was being amassed, even if they weren't showing themselves yet.

She turned back to the glass tube. Her brother's eyes slowly opened, and he blinked a few times, his pupils not yet focused. Alex touched the panel a few more times, and the glass split down the middle before curving away underneath her brother, leaving him open to the world again.

His eyes found her. There was knowledge in them. He was remembering faster than she had. "Is it finished?"

"Yes," she said with tears in her eyes.

"Where is the other version of me?" Alexander asked.

Alex said nothing, only turned her head to the right. The glass tube was there, the person inside silent. Slowly, Alexander turned his body off the stretcher he lay on. His muscles were unlike anything she'd ever seen, each fiber and vein detailed beneath the flesh. He didn't seem to mind or even notice that he was naked in front of his sister.

He let his feet touch the floor and tested his legs. He didn't collapse as Alex had done but was able to hold himself up. His first step was awkward, but by the second, his body was adapting *quickly. He crossed the space between him and the other version. Alex walked behind him, remaining a few feet away.*

He looked down into the glass tube. Very carefully, he placed his massive hands on the glass. Alex had no delusions about what those hands could do. Breaking that tube would be as simple for him as it had been for her, perhaps even simpler.

"Which one is the original?" he asked without turning around. "Do you know?"

"No," Alex whispered.

"Should I kill him?"

Alex shook her head in confusion. The thought had never occurred to her. She'd felt sorrow for the other version of her, not malice.

"I don't know, Alexander. Why would you?"

Her brother continued looking through the glass. "Because he might kill me one day. Maybe today when he wakes."

"I'd leave him alone," she responded. "There are more pressing things to worry about."

Her brother was quiet for a few moments, then nodded. "Maybe you're right." He tapped the glass softly, then turned. His eyes didn't focus on his sister but behind her. "Why are you here?"

Alex realized she could sense the other people in the room. She'd missed them coming in because she'd been focused on her brother, but now? She knew how many were here before she turned to look.

Her father's second in charge had come. Spurius de Docilus, a man she'd known since she was a child. He'd seen much war but was also meticulous in his administrative duties. He was not someone to trifle with, and like her father in the other medbay, he showed no fear now.

"I'm here," Spurius said, "because neither of you is supposed to be awake, let alone out of your capsules." He walked closer to them but remained a few yards away. "What you did in the other medbay, Alexandria, was inexcusable. Your father is still unconscious."

Alexander cocked his head to the side as he looked at his sister. "What did you do?"

Spurious laughed. "She attacked the Praetorian Guard and then her father. Killed a man upstairs, too."

Alexander's eyes widened. "Why?"

"Because neither of you is supposed to be awake yet. The procedures aren't finished."

Alexander looked at Spurius. "Is my father injured?"

"He's certainly worse off than when he woke up this morning." Spurius stepped closer. "I need the two of you to do nothing else, not leave this medbay, and let us get you back into the capsules." His glance at Alex was full of disgust. "We'll have to get another one brought in for you. Do you both understand?"

Alexandria understood no such thing. She wasn't going into any more capsules. She wasn't letting them do another damned thing to her, regardless of what her father or this man wanted.

She stepped away from her brother. "No, I don't think I will, Spurius. I think you should go back to wherever it is you came from, at least if you want to continue moving like you do now."

Spurius sighed and looked at Alexander. "Is the answer the same for you?"

"What isn't finished with the procedure?" her brother asked.

Alex looked at him. "You can't be serious."

He didn't glance at her but kept his eyes on Spurius. "Answer me."

"Am I a doctor, Alexander? I only know what I've been told

and the obvious results she has shown since being released. Murder and mayhem are running rampant within these walls right now, and the doctors say you aren't ready to be out." He shook his head as he stared at Alex again. "Something happened during her procedure, and it woke her up. Then, of course, she comes here and lets you out. None of this is how it should have gone."

Alexander rubbed a massive hand through his hair. His nakedness didn't appear to bother him, as if he were beyond such things. Alex knew her brother was never modest, but something was different about him now. "Spurius," he said, "I don't think I want to get back in the capsule. I rather like how I feel right now."

Spurius took a deep breath. He'd come alone, and he understood there wasn't anything he could do to these two new specimens. "Is this really how you both want it? You are de Finitas. Your father is ordering you back into the capsule. Not me. Not his Titans or Guard. Him. The man who conquered the solar system. Do you both want to go against his wishes?"

"Father isn't here," Alex said. "It's just the three of us, and I'm tired of talking with you."

When her brother spoke, it was like he hadn't heard either of the other two. "I'll go to my father and see what he wants."

Spurius' eyes narrowed. "He isn't conscious, Alexander."

Her brother began walking then, passing Spurius and heading to the stairs that led out of the medbay.

A moment later, Alex and Spurius were left with the second version of her brother.

He looked at Alex. "Do you see? Surely you can tell something isn't right with him. Do you see what you've done?"

Alex closed her eyes. It was an odd feeling, something she

hadn't experienced. She and her brother had always been close in a way other people couldn't understand. They could tell what the other was feeling even when not in the same room. They knew when something important had happened to the other despite not being told. This was different.

She could see her brother. He was walking up the second flight of stairs, his thigh muscles bulging against his skin with each step. She blocked out the room she stood in and focused on her brother. She could see more than his feelings now. She was able to see his thoughts. It was as though she lived in his brain.

He's different, she realized. Either that or I never knew him at all.

Alex knew he could feel her there. She sensed no surprise in him, though, as if he'd known that was coming.

She'd known her brother had something of an ego and was arrogant. She'd thought two things about it, the first being that such arrogance might come naturally when one's father conquered the known universe. The second was that the arrogance might mask underlying insecurities.

As she remained in his brain, a stark realization fell over her: Alexander de Finita, the first of his name, had no insecurities. No part of his mind doubted anything. There were no shadows of insecurities hiding in the recesses. Here was a man so supremely convinced of his rightness that anything or anyone who disagreed with him must cease to exist.

Alex's mouth opened slightly, her eyes widening in fear as she realized the gravity of her last thought.

Anything or anyone who disagreed with him must cease to exist.

Alex closed her eyes and shook her head, trying to clear these strange thoughts. She paused her search for a moment, not caring *about the other man in the room with her. Alexander had changed, but surely not that much. What she'd seen inside her brother's head hadn't been human. It was alien.*

Spurius must have known something was happening in front of him because he said nothing, nor did he dare touch Alex.

With her eyes still closed, she dove back into her brother's mind.

Can you hear me, Sister?

It was Alexander's voice. She could hear him...thinking? That wasn't quite it, but close. They were connected somehow, and he was speaking to her.

I know you can. You and I are heading toward our fate. Can you feel it?

It was the first time he had used the word fate. Alex had no idea what he was talking about, this huge man now stomping naked through the castle. I'm going to see our father, *her brother continued,* then you and I will continue our journey together.

Alex opened her eyes, practically fleeing her brother's mind. Spurius stared at her with fear on his face. She saw that he understood what had been done to her, even if she didn't. He had been in on the plans like her brother and father. Watching her just then with her eyes closed, he probably had a good idea of what she'd been doing.

"What did you do to me?" *Alex demanded.*

"I didn't do anything. This wasn't my plan, Alexandria. I serve at the pleasure of the Ascendant. You know this." *The man's entire demeanor had changed in a few moments.* "This wasn't my plan."

"Tell me what you did to me, Spurius. Now."

Alexander de Finita, first of his name, never imagined that such a change could have happened. Before he woke up as this new creature, he had lived a life in someone else's shadow—his father's. It spread over and beyond him. No matter how hard Alexander had tried to run, that shadow remained, covering him. He'd known that unless something drastic happened, he'd never be more than his father's son.

That was why he agreed to the modification. He understood his sister's fears, but without such an operation, his legacy would never be greater than Aurelius de Finita's.

As he approached his father, a revelation came to him. He knew his whole life—indeed, the entire universe's arc—had led to this very moment. Alexander had been reborn, and with his rebirth came a new era.

He felt his sister enter his mind. He was not surprised to find himself able to speak to her. He had known the plans for both of them, though Alexandria hadn't. He felt her shock and disgust at what she found inside his mind. She didn't yet understand; the revelation had not come to her, but in time, it would.

In time, all would see as Alexander now did.

He made it to just outside his father's private medical room.

The remaining Praetorian Guard stood in front of the double doors. Their faces were guarded inside their MechSuits, but it was clear the five guarding his father didn't know what to do. They most likely had orders that no one could see the Imperial Ascendant. They also knew about the botched modifications and that Alexandria was running around the First Residence killing people.

With all that going on, a naked Imperial Ascendant Rising, the next in line for the Ascendancy, stood in front of them.

A changed Ascendant Rising as well. One who was a perfect human specimen, even beyond human.

"I wish to see my father," Alexander stated.

The middle guard spoke, his voice projecting strength through the MechSuit's speaker. "I'm sorry, my liege. No one is allowed to see the Ascendant."

The Guard didn't draw their weapons. Despite his obvious physical strength, the man in front of them was naked and had no weapon of his own. To draw on the Ascendant Rising was a capital offense.

"Part ways and let me pass or die," Alexander instructed. "I don't care which you choose."

"My liege, no one is allowed to enter."

Alexander stepped forward, and his massive hand took hold of the guard's helmet. He squeezed, and the metal was like an orange's skin beneath his fingers. The guard had no time to raise his Whip, his skull cracking beneath the immense pressure. Alexander released him, and he fell to the floor.

He turned to the rest. These were not easily frightened men, not bureaucrats or senators. These were men who had made it through the Academy and fought their way to the upper echelon of warriors. They looked at their fallen comrade, his metal-encased legs twitching as his nervous system slowly shut down, and spread out.

Whips unfurled from their hands.

They did not serve the Ascendant Rising but the Ascendant, and an attack on his Praetorian Guard was an attack on him.

Alexander did not care. He had given them a choice, and they had chosen wrong. Now they would die. He looked at the floor,

DAVID BEERS & MICHAEL ANDERLE

his hands turning to fists. Even in their MechSuits, the Guard were smaller than the man in front of them.

They came for him as one, their training teaching them how to cut a man down before he could move.

Alexander was the only one in this outer room who knew he was no longer a man. He had become something superior, an evolution.

He grabbed the first Praetorian's fighting arm, seizing the wrist as he dodged the Whip. He wrenched the guard's arm up, and there was the scream of metal as it bent and was sheared from its base. It was accompanied by the screams that boomed out over the suit's speaker.

Alexander ripped the man's arm off his body, metal, flesh, and bone. The Whip fell to the ground inert. He did not slow but spun as he ducked and slammed the detached arm into the knee of his pursuer. The knee bent and then snapped, the guard collapsing to the floor as another scream was added to the cacophony.

A Whip slashed for Alexander's head, but he pulled back, his reflexes faster than even a MechSuit. The Guard who had swiped at him wasn't able to raise his Whip in time, and the savaged metal arm pulverized his head and neck.

His head bent unnaturally to the right, nearly touching his shoulder. He stood for a few moments before his legs gave out and he hit the floor.

Only one remained, but he'd fallen back. His Whip was between him and Alexander, but both knew it didn't matter. No Whip could stop this new type of creature.

"I wish to see my father," Alexander stated again.

The Praetorian's Whip retracted into the hilt, and he took a step back.

Alexander nodded at the man. He knew that once he stepped through the double doors, this guard would call for backup. Alexander didn't care. What he'd just done to this group only solidified what he felt in his bones: he was the future.

He turned to the doors. They opened for his body's signature, and he walked into his father's room. A human doctor stood against the far wall, his hands shaking in front of him. He held no weapon, not even a scalpel, and he knew what had just happened outside this room. "Please don't hurt me," he whispered.

Alexander looked at his father lying on the bed in the middle of the room. His face was badly bruised, purple and black from his sister's attack. He stepped closer to the table and didn't look at the doctor as he said, "Leave us."

The doctor scurried from the room as fast as possible. Alexander was left alone with his father.

He knew the man was awake.

"Have you come to finish what your sister started?" Aurelius asked without opening his eyes. His voice was weak, strained. Alexander had never seen his father in such a condition, but his heart held no sympathy.

"Why are we different, Father?" he asked. "She and I were supposed to be the same mentally and physically. That was the plan. We're not, though."

"One of my children wanted nothing, and one wanted it all," Aurelius muttered. "I made you different because neither of you should have all the power in the universe. If you want to conquer everything, you'll need one another now."

"You're a fool, Father. She's stronger than I am. She can do things I can't, so tell me, how are you going to stop her when she comes here to finish the job on you? I can't stop her. All of your

Praetorian Guards and Titans can't stop her. What are you going to do?"

"Things are in motion that you're not aware of, Alexander. Soon, though, you'll see the light. I promise."

Alexander felt the change in airflow a moment before he heard the doors opening. He turned his body gracefully, ready to kill whatever was at the door.

Before he could move, ten syringes fired in a tight pattern flew through the air and punctured his torso. Alexander looked down, blinking as some kind of subduing agent pumped into his bloodstream. He looked up and saw his attacker at the other end of the waiting room. The Guard he'd let flee held a pump-action weapon with ten holes in the business end.

Alexander took a step toward him, fighting off the effects of the needles with all his might. He took another step, reaching down to the syringes as he did. He ripped out five with one giant hand, scattering them on the floor. The mighty Alexander took one more step, then swayed on his feet. He reached forward with his hand as if he could stretch across the floor to his enemy and bring him down.

Alexander tried taking one more step, but his leg gave out, and he collapsed.

His father never once opened his eyes.

Alex looked down at her hands. They were shaking, and she didn't know how long they'd been doing that.

In a rush, Spurius had told her what they'd done, but she'd made him slow down and repeat it. She wanted to be clear on what was different about her, and she also wanted to know if she was the clone.

They had attempted something new with her. All of the other experiments had revolved around physical modifications. She'd had the first mental modification. They hadn't known if it would work in reality, only theoretically.

"What about my brother?" she asked.

"What about him?"

Alex found the man's eyes. "Did he want the mental modification, or did he leave that for me?"

"I...I don't know."

She knew he was lying, but she didn't push that any further.

"What was our father's plan for us?" Alex asked. "I know it wasn't what he told our brother, to conquer the rest of the galaxy. Why did he do this?"

Spurius looked shocked at the question. "What do you mean? Why would he do this if not to allow humanity to stretch its arm farther into the universe?"

Alex understood later that the question had been meant to do exactly what it did: take her mind off what was around her. She quit focusing on her surroundings, on her mind's new ability to see around corners, and considered that her father might have been telling the truth.

The pain was sharp and precise as multiple needles punctured her back at the same time. Alex's eyes widened as she realized what was happening. Her mind pulled them from her back almost as quickly as they'd sliced into her. She was too late, though. The payload had been delivered.

She stared at Spurius; the man's scared attitude was gone. He was smiling and nodding. He'd known, and Alex had been naive to trust this man not to be plotting something else. She'd been too confident in these new abilities she didn't truly understand.

"Goodnight, Alexandria," Spurius said.

Alex fell to the floor, just as her brother had in a different room.

Alex's eyes opened.

Something was in her mouth.

No, something had been shoved down her throat. She started to choke, trying to gag up whatever was inside her. It wouldn't move, though. Next, she felt her eyes burning bright and hot, realizing quickly that she was floating in some kind of liquid. Tubes had also been shoved into her nose, keeping her from breathing in whatever surrounded her. She tried to raise her hand to wipe her eyes, but she felt the clamps.

They held both her wrists and ankles.

Where was she?

The liquid surrounding her had a blue tint to it, although it obviously wasn't water. It took Alex a second, but she began to calm herself. She closed her eyes against the burning fluid and forced down the panic the tubes in her body brought out. She searched with her newly powerful mind, needing to understand what was around her in a way her other senses couldn't describe

Her father's voice broke through her concentration. "There's no need for that, darling."

She opened her eyes but was only met with that same burn. She couldn't see outside the liquid, and as she tried to mentally push past the barriers holding her and this fluid in, she realized she couldn't.

"You threatened everything I've been building, Alexandria. Not to mention you killed a lot of good men. You almost killed me, too."

Alex didn't know where her father was. His voice came from everywhere at once, and she could see nothing.

"There's no sense in using the modifications that you so desperately didn't want. They're nullified right now due to the liquid you're floating in. They're going to remain nullified for the rest of time, too. Or at least until we can get a better handle on what went wrong. The other version of you hasn't woken up yet, so we don't know how the experiment has played out."

Alex stopped struggling. She stopped trying to find her father or figure out what exactly was happening. She allowed herself to float with her eyes closed. Where was her brother? Was he suspended in something like this as well, or had her father looked more kindly on him?

"I listened to Alexander's plan when maybe I shouldn't have. Or at least I listened to it partly. What he wanted was for the two of you to have both modifications, the mental and physical. That was never going to happen, but I was interested to see if we could do it." Her father sighed, and although Alex couldn't see him, she felt the resignation in his voice. The knowledge of his failure.

"Another change was supposed to take place in both of you, but I think the reverse happened. Either that or the change simply didn't complete itself. That's why I'm tempted to see what happens with the other you, whether or not the change takes place. You both were supposed to be more...suggestible. Envoys who would conquer the galaxy at my behest, not overthrow me."

Her father paused, and for the first time, Alex felt a deep pang of sorrow for him. Not anger, not hate, but pity. He had sacrificed his two children to his never-ending quest for domination. She knew without asking that he would have another heir, one who would rule from the throne while his first male heir was sent out as basically a robot killer. Her? What had Alex's purpose been in all this? She didn't need to read the man's mind to know. Alex had only been an experiment. Her father had wanted to know whether it would be possible to modify her mentally.

Now he knew.

So he'd put her in this vat of liquid and come down here to hear himself speak. To let her know she had lost, despite her rage and power.

"Maybe I'll try again," her father mused from somewhere beyond Alex's vat. "Or maybe my successor will have to do that. Perhaps our technology isn't advanced enough yet."

Had he ever loved them? Had her ever been capable of love? Or was the need for conquest all that filled this man?

"You won't try again, Aurelius."

The pity running through Alex's mind screeched to a halt. That had been her mother's voice, and she sounded neither exhausted nor drunk. Alex reflexively opened her eyes, and while they burned again, the blue tint was fading from the liquid. It was as if the coloring was being drained out somehow, and Alex was able to see out of the vat. The more transparent the liquid became, the better she could see.

Alex had never been in this room before. She didn't even know where it was, whether they were still at the Imperial Residence or somewhere else. Her mother stood at the back of the room, while her father sat in a chair directly in front of the vat. Alex turned her head to the left and saw that the other version of her was similarly suspended, though her eyes were closed.

She didn't see her brother anywhere.

Her eyes went to her mother again. Her father hadn't even

bothered standing from his chair, only turned halfway around to look at his wife.

"What are you doing here, woman?" he asked, sounding more tired than Alex had ever heard him. "Did you manage to quit drinking long enough to venture out of bed?"

Alex finally saw the weapon in her mother's hand. It was something new that her father's scientists had invented. Alex had seen prototypes, but never one in the wild. It was supposed to produce a laser beam like something out of the science fiction stories from a hundred years before. She held it with two hands, pointing it directly at Alex's father.

"You're going to let her go, Aurelius. What you've done is beyond disgraceful. It's alien. Disgusting." Her mother shook her head and spat on the floor. "It ends now. All this insanity ends now."

Alex couldn't remember the last time she'd seen her mother with such spirit. The woman had been a drunk who lived like the ostrich of old, head buried in the sand.

Not anymore, Alex thought.

"You think I do this for me?" Aurelius asked, still not bothering to stand. "You think I give up my own flesh and blood for myself? You are a foolish woman. Perhaps even a stupid woman. I don't do this for myself. I do this for mankind. Everything I've done, from the moment I started this conquest, has been to create peace. Before me, mankind were brutes. After me, they will have peace forever."

Her mother spat again. "I've been listening to that bullshit for years, Aurelius. I've been listening to you tell anyone who would listen about how selfless you are and how much you care. What about the cities that you claim had nuclear bombs detonated in them? Do you tell anyone what you're doing in those cities?"

Her father stood at that. He glanced around the room as if to reassure himself that they were alone. Alex knew what her mother was talking about. The nuclear explosions had happened in major cities across the globe, right before her father had started his almost miraculous ascent. The areas were too hot for anyone to live near, let alone go into.

"If you want to continue living, woman, shut your mouth," her father said, his voice suddenly full of simmering rage. "You speak of things you have no right to know, and you quicken the end of your life with each new syllable you utter."

Alex's mother smiled, a cruel twist of her lips Alex had never before witnessed. "Do you think you can scare me, Aurelius? We both know you cannot harm me. Regardless of what you do to the rest of the men in this world, I am untouchable. Your life will be forfeit."

Her father smiled back. "And what do you think killing me will do? Do you think you'll just march back upstairs and continue living?"

"I don't care about my life, Aurelius. I've already sacrificed it by marrying you, by listening to my father, by purchasing royalty with my soul." She shook her head without taking her eyes off her husband. "No, I don't care anymore. What I do care about is you letting Alexandria out of that contraption right now. Then we'll talk about my son and what can be done there."

"That's not your daughter. It's a clone. Your daughter is the one still asleep. The one I can't wake up."

Alex's mother laughed. "You can lie to the rest of your flunkies, but you can't fool a mother about her daughter. The clone hasn't woken yet, and maybe it never will. It doesn't matter what you copied over; you weren't able to replicate the full being. My children woke, but the others haven't. Now, Aurelius, am I going to have to kill you for you to free her? Is that really what we've come to?"

Alex remembered this version of her mother, but it had been so long since she'd seen her. Her father's personality and drive had almost erased this woman from existence.

"You're not going to kill me, so put the weapon down," her father instructed.

Her mother took five rapid steps across the room and fired the laser. She didn't have great aim, but it seared the side of Aurelius's leg. He went down to one knee with a deep groan and looked up at his wife, rage on his face. "You fucking bitch. Put the weapon down now, or I'm going to kill you myself. The consequences be damned."

Her mother kept a healthy distance from Aurelius, knowing how fast and strong the man could be, even weakened. "You're almost out of time. I've got an internal clock going, and it started the moment I walked into this room. I won't be here all day because I can kill you and let her go. I know that. It might cost me more in the end, but I can deal with that. So, do you want to still be here when this is all over, or would you rather me go ahead and take you out?"

The blue tint inside the liquid was gone now. Alex could see everything clearly. Something was still blocking her from using her modifications, so she supposed it hadn't been the blue tint in the liquid. Her mother must have somehow been able to drain that, but releasing Alex was beyond her abilities.

Alex could see part of her father's face, rage still on it, but she also saw resignation. His leg was bleeding profusely, and he couldn't reach his wife from where he knelt. Perhaps he saw something in his wife, too—a truth that meant she would kill him if he didn't do as she wanted.

"AI," he said to the room.

"Yes, my liege?" the computer responded.

"Release the human who is awake." His voice shook with anger.

"Please confirm directive," the AI responded.

"Release the conscious human," her father said from the floor, still staring at his wife with unadulterated hatred.

The liquid around Alex slowly started to flow downward, emptying from some unseen tube. She felt it passing over the top of her skull, then moving down her face. The clamps on her wrists and ankles released, and she found herself able to move. She was floating in the liquid but slowly moving to the bottom of the vat.

Outside, her mother kept the weapon pointed at her father. She didn't glance at the vat, knowing that to give Aurelius a moment's inattention would surely mean death.

Finally, Alex's feet touched the bottom. There was a painful moment as the throat and nose tubes wrenched themselves out of her face. She fell to her knees, gagging. The stalemate continued outside. Her mother still didn't glance at her.

The vat's glass walls retracted into the platform beneath, leaving Alex naked as she stared at her parents. She remained on her knees but knew her abilities had returned.

Her mother didn't look at her as she spoke. "Go, Alexandria. Lucia is waiting for you. Do as she says. I'll deal with your father."

Lucia was her mother's assistant, loyal only to her mother. Alex understood she could be trusted.

She stood up and carefully climbed off the platform. Her muscles were weak. She wasn't sure how long she'd been in the *vat, but she would need to be careful when it came to moving quickly.*

She walked over to her father. He was still on the floor, though he managed to hold himself up.

His eyes remained on her mother as he spoke to her. "You don't know what you're doing, Alexandria. You have no idea how deadly things are going to get for you if you walk out that door. Your mother doesn't know either. She's a fool, and she's been a fool most of your life. You know that. You've watched her lounge around in bed for years. Why listen to her now?"

"Go, Alexandria," her mother instructed. "Preparations have been made, but there isn't much time. He won't follow you for a while yet."

Alex looked at her father on the floor. She wanted to say something, but she couldn't find any words that described what she now felt toward the man. Instead, naked and still wet, she turned away and walked toward the door her mother had entered through.

It was the last time she would see her father in person.

Or her mother.

Alexander watched his parents walk into the room with surprise. Minutes before, he'd been surrounded by a blue-tinted liquid that burned his eyes, although his skin felt okay. Tubes were stuffed down his throat and nose, and clamps kept his arms and legs from freeing him. He'd tried pulling against them but had gotten nowhere. To his left was the other version of himself, the one he hadn't yet killed. It still didn't seem to be awake, however.

He remembered what had happened to bring him here, the syringes that had skewered his midsection, but nothing after that.

At some point, the blue tint had begun to fade from the liquid surrounding Alexander. He'd forced his eyes open against the burn to see what was occurring. Minutes passed, but eventually, his father had hobbled in. A deep burn penetrated his thigh, and Alexander could see fluid still weeping from it.

His mother came in behind him. She was holding one of the new StarBeams with both hands. She had it pointed at his father's back, although she was smart enough to remain a safe distance away. He carried no weapons, and Alexander recognized that had been his mistake, a stupid one that had cost him more than he could have imagined.

What is it you want to do, Mother? Alexander wondered in the still-clearing vat.

"Release him," she demanded.

"You are a stupid, stupid woman," Aurelius responded. "Do you have any idea what you're doing right now? The girl was bad enough, but you want me to release him?"

She fired a warning shot close to his other leg, and the laser singed his pants before it struck the floor. Aurelius quickly brushed his leg with his hand, putting out the fire. He made no noise and did not turn to look at his wife, only kept his eyes on Alexander. "AI, release the human who is awake."

"Please confirm, my liege," the AI responded.

"Release the human who is awake."

A minute or two passed while the liquid drained from the vat and the clamps released Alexander. He grunted as the tubes were pulled out of his head, but he remained standing. These two in front of him had no idea what was happening, nor what was to *happen, and he understood that. He stepped down from the platform and looked at his mother. "Where is Alexandria?"*

"She's gone, Alexander. What do you want with her?"

He hadn't seen his mother be this forceful in many years. Perhaps when he was a child, she'd been like this, but it had been a long time. "She's my sister, and I need to talk to her. Where is she, Mother?"

"She's gone, Alexander. It's very important that you answer me honestly. What do you want with your sister?"

Do you know, Mother? *he wondered.* Or do you only have your suspicions?

He stepped slowly across the room and stopped in front of his father. Up close, he could see the pain coursing through the man. The pain was taking its toll, and Alexander wondered how long he could remain standing like this. "I need her. He has made it so that I need her." He glanced over his father's shoulder at his mother. "You know that, though, don't you? Is it your intuition, or were you in on this from the beginning?"

"You can't have her, Alexander. Neither you nor your father. What you've both done to her is sickening beyond words, and it stops now. She's leaving, and the two of you... I don't even know where to begin."

Alexander stepped around his father, not worried about what the old man might do to him. He was to the right of the Star-Beam, which remained pointed at Aurelius, who was about a yard away from his mother. "Where did you send Alexandria?"

"It's none of your concern. She's out of your reach now. Yours and his."

Alexander would think back to the next moment as the years passed and his body changed. He would grow older, he and his sister both, far outliving both their parents and the descendants

41

who would come. Indeed, the descendants who came after Alexander would only be half-bloods because of Alexander's next action.

He moved too fast for his mother to react. One moment she held the StarBeam, and the next, it was in her son's hand.

She remained where she was, mouth open in shock. Her eyes were wide, and her hands remained as they'd been when she was holding the weapon.

"Where did you send my sister?" Alexander asked.

"I'm not going to tell you. Whatever you've become, you and your father, I'm not going to let you pull her into it any more than you already have."

Alexander smiled. She only partly understood, but she was missing the most important piece. "Mother, Alexandria has no choice in the matter. Neither do you. Neither does my father. Everything has already been arranged."

His mother's face twisted in confusion.

Alexander pulled the trigger.

The confusion turned to surprise and pain. His mother looked down at the wound in her gut. The laser had cut straight through her, leaving a cauterized hole.

She fell to her knees, reaching out to try to stabilize herself on him. He stepped back before her hands could touch him, and she hit both knees hard. He heard his father move. Alexander swung his left hand back and grabbed him by the head, then tossed him toward the wall. The man hit the floor and skidded until he smashed into a table.

Everything on top of it fell on his father. Alexander stared at him for a few moments while his mother gasped at his feet. Aurelius didn't move. Alexander thought he was only pretending to be unconscious. It didn't matter. He had to find Alexandria.

He had to make this transition complete to fulfill what must be done.

He looked down at his mother. She was curled in a fetal position. She was most likely in shock, unaware of her surroundings. Alexander knelt and touched her back softly. "I'm sorry. There are things that must happen, and you were in the way of them. I promise you won't be the last, and I promise your death won't be in vain."

His mother gave another gasp as her right hand twitched involuntarily. Alexander stood up and glanced once more at his father. He should probably kill the man too, but he couldn't quite bring himself to do it. Despite the treachery, his father had made all this possible. Alexander left him under the equipment covering him and walked out of the room.

He had to find his sister before his mother's plans got in the way.

Lucia had given Alex a robe and wrapped it around her as they scurried away from her parents. She kept expecting to hear another shot fired or a scream, but she heard nothing of the kind —just the echo of their feet as they moved through empty hallways. Alex didn't know how they could be empty, why her father didn't have more protection, and assumed her mother must have fixed that problem.

"Where are we going?" she asked Lucia.

The assistant was leading the way, draped in fear that covered her much as did her clothing. "To a ship. I'm to get you off the planet."

Alex stopped then and took Lucia by the shoulder. "What do you mean by 'off the planet?' Where am I going?" She'd thought her mother would get her out of the Imperial Residence, but off Earth? That was overkill. Alex wasn't leaving.

"I don't know where the ship is taking you. Your mother made sure no one would know. We've got to hurry." Lucia looked at both ends of the hallway, likely expecting Praetorians to arrive at any second.

Alex loosened her grip on the woman's shoulder. "It's okay. I can sense if anyone's coming. We're alone right now. Now, why did my mother tell you I had to get off the planet?"

Lucia finally met her gaze. "She didn't tell me why, Alexandria. She only said that was what I was to do. We must hurry. Do you understand?"

Alex could tell that disobeying her mother's orders would cause Lucia untold mental anguish, and she didn't want that. They would go to the ship, and then Alex could find out exactly what was happening. "Okay, take me there."

The walk to the first transport was a long one. Alex used the time to test the talents she'd been given. She stretched her mind throughout the premises, finding that they were beneath the Imperial Residence. She spread out from there, her sight taking her down hallways. She saw a completely new "Imperial Residence." The space beneath the ground was at least as large as the structure atop it, yet Alex had never seen it. Never heard about it.

Another of her father's secrets.

They arrived at the transport, and Alex felt real fear. She saw that her mother had directed her father to Alexander's place of confinement. The transport waited in front of her, ready to take her to the ship that would get her off Earth. Alex closed her eyes and watched as her mother marched her father into the room that contained Alexander.

Why was she scared? She'd never feared Alexander before. Other people had, and for good reason, but not her. Yet, she didn't want him to get out of that vat. Whatever her mother was doing right now, Alex felt sure it was the wrong decision. She opened her eyes and found Lucia staring anxiously at her. "We have to go back."

The assistant looked at Alex as if she'd suddenly sprouted a second head and it was speaking alien gibberish. "We can't, Alexandria. You have to get on the transport now. I can't disobey your mother. You know this. Neither of us can."

She closed her eyes for a brief second and saw they were arguing. She could hear them if she tried, but Lucia started shaking her, pulling her from her vision. "Alexandria, we have to go now."

Alex's face grew confused. "You're coming."

"Yes." The assistant nodded. "I'm to go with you wherever you go."

Alex didn't understand, but the fear inside her grew with each passing second. She could go back underground and try to stop whatever her mother was about to do, but this woman would follow her. She had served her mother loyally for too many years to disregard an order. Alex thought she could protect herself despite the increasing fear, but someone else? No.

"Please, Alexandria," Lucia begged. "We have to go."

Alex didn't know what else to do, so she stepped into the transport. Lucia rushed in after her and stood in front of the door until it closed. She didn't say anything, but Alex knew the woman was ensuring that she would have to knock her over to escape.

The transport took off, and Alex watched the Imperial Residence grow smaller as they soared into the sky. She half-expected to see attack transports chasing them in the darkness, but there were none. Just the night sky and clouds to greet them.

Long minutes passed, then Alex felt him. She and her brother had always had a strong connection, but this was something altogether different. As the transport raced toward the ship, her ability to see inside the Residence had diminished until it disappeared.

And yet, she felt her brother. He wasn't in a transport chasing her, but he was out of the vat.

She closed her eyes, though she didn't want to go to him. She didn't want to see what he was doing, though she didn't know why.

"Are you okay, Alexandria?" Lucia asked.

Alex nodded. She kept her eyes closed, not reaching for her brother but so overwhelmed by the connection that she wasn't sure what else she could do.

"We're almost there," the assistant said.

Alex looked out the window at the dock. Compared to the last time she'd seen it, it was deserted. A small ship sat poised to take off, one that could only hold twenty passengers at most. Alex saw no one else around it, no dock workers, no engineers. It must have also been her mother's doing. Somehow, this had been planned in detail. Alex hadn't known her mother was capable of it.

Their transport touched down two hundred yards from the ship. Alex had no intention of getting on it. However, there would be a pilot on board, and she could find out exactly where he planned on taking her.

Alex stepped off the transport into the cold night air and was nearly rocked off her feet. She shut her eyes tight and grabbed the transport's side.

Where are you going, Sister?

She didn't know how he was speaking to her, but the force of his words had nearly brought her to her knees.

"Alexandria!" *Lucia called. Alex could only shake her head in response.*

I can't see you, *Alexander continued.* But I can feel you. Whatever they've done to us, they've brought us closer in that way.

What have you done? *Alex replied. She could tell something was different, but not what. He was hiding it from her somehow.*

I killed our mother, *Alexander responded.* It had to happen, Alexandria. She saw what must be done but didn't have the stomach to do it, so she had to die.

Alex had never considered her mother's mortality. She'd always been there, even at her worst. You're lying, *she whispered in her mind.*

You know I'm not, *came the cold response.*

Alex slid down, and her ass hit concrete. Lucia rushed to her, and Alex opened her eyes. The ship was still waiting in the distance. Alex couldn't manage to say anything to the woman squatting over her, desperate to know what was wrong.

Where are you going, Alexandria? *her brother asked.* We are not finished here. You and I have more to do.

He was coming for her. Alex felt that in her bones. He said he couldn't see her, but she knew he felt her well enough.

She's dead? *Alex asked.* Truly?

You know she is. Reach out for her. Feel her. Can you?

There was nothing, no sense of her mother. A gut-wrenching sorrow took over, causing tears to flow down her cheeks. Lucia was pulling on her, trying to get her to stand. Alex couldn't pay attention to any of it. Her mother had risked her life to come and save Alex, and she'd ended up giving it to her son, whom she'd also come to save.

What has become of you, Alexander? *she asked through her sobbing.*

She was on her feet, being dragged toward the ship.

I am heading toward my fate, my destiny. As are you. Come back to me, Alexandria. We must become one. Surely you see this. We are already connected in a way no humans have been before. We must finish this connection.

Alex blinked away tears and watched as the ship got closer. She knew what her brother meant even if he didn't spell it out. He would throw her in another vat, and there he'd figure out how to join the two of them.

He would take her mind from her and put it in him.

Then what?

Come to me, Alexandria. This is our fate, *he whispered, and she knew he was after her. Still naked, he'd gotten into his own transport and was heading for the docks. He was coming to stop her.*

"Alexandria, hurry. We don't have much time," *Lucia begged as she pulled on Alex's arm. Lucia couldn't know what her brother intended, but she understood the docks wouldn't be empty forever. Her mother's power only stretched so far. Or it had.*

She blinked through tears, looking from Lucia to the ship. If her brother arrived here, could she stop him? Alex had no idea. Physically, no one had ever existed like him. Even the myth of Samson couldn't live up to what her brother had become.

And Lucia? She would die, just like her mother. Anyone else who ventured onto the docks? Dead.

If Alex lost? She didn't know if what her brother wanted was possible, but if he achieved it? The solar system would be his, if not the entire universe.

That was what made up her mind. It was what sent her away from Earth and changed the entire history of the human species. It was what brought Alistair Kane to Pluto a thousand years later, separating him from his love and starting an Insurrection that would shake the very universe.

CHAPTER FOUR

The AllMother was seated. Her story has taken the better part of a few hours.

"His warped dream has never ceased," she said. "Even now, a thousand years later, he hunts me to take whatever they implanted in me."

Alistair remained lying on his cot and staring up at the ceiling. His eyes were narrow as he considered what he'd just heard. "It doesn't make any sense. There are too many logical issues here to overlook."

The AllMother's voice sounded tired, but she waved him on. "Ask your questions."

"The first is, how have you both lived so long?"

"I can't speak for Alexander, only myself. My modifications allowed me to prolong my life. My mental abilities aren't just limited to what I see here and now. I can send my mind into the future. I can avoid things that would hurt me. I can also repair my cells in a way that's impossible for normal humans, even with all the medical advances that have come about. Or I could. All of these things I'm telling you were possible at one time, although my abilities are fading quickly."

"And your brother?" Alistair asked.

"I can't say for certain. I imagine it has to do with his modification, but while I spent my time building a movement, he spent his time perfecting his modifications. Through trial and error, he created those Myrmidons in his image."

Alistair ran his hands through his hair as he considered the next question. "Why you? If he's perfected his modifications, and he understands how to create *your* type of modification, the mental kind, why is he waiting for you?"

"You're making assumptions that I don't think are true," she responded. "I'm not sure he knows how to replicate my modification without me. Before you, no one else in the universe, as far as I'm aware, had modifications like mine. It took me a longer time than I'll admit to figure out how to do it, and the Commonwealth never tried again, as far as I can tell. I'm not sure how he plans to do it, but it'll probably be some sort of mapping and then overlaying it on his modifications." She paused for a brief second. "There's more to it, however. Whether he's insane or not, I don't know. But to his mind, it's *our* genetic lineage that must rule. He would never settle for something other than his own sister's pairing with him. If he'd ever considered such a thing, perhaps he would have already won."

Alistair had heard her story, and there was much more that he hadn't yet heard. "What happened to Lucia?"

The AllMother smiled at that, and her eyes grew hazy. "She died a long time ago. My life-extension powers don't extend to others, unfortunately. She served me as loyally as she had my mother, though."

Finally, Alistair got to the question that mattered most. "I'm not like you, am I? In a way, I am, but I don't have the control that you did when you first awoke. What I did was out of necessity, to keep me alive. You can control it. You can venture into people's minds and see around corners. You can break people's legs as they step. I can't do those things. I'm a bomb waiting to go off."

"Maybe it *is* my genetics," the AllMother said. "But yes, there are differences between us. I know, though, that even at my greatest, I couldn't do what you did. I couldn't defeat an entire army with a single burst."

"Do you know what I will become?"

"All I know is that you're the one leading us back to Earth, Prometheus. What you become? That's up to you." The old woman stood, tired from speaking so much. "If my brother gets hold of me, that's what he's going to do. If he can do it, he may become unstoppable. Before that happens, you should kill me. Do you understand?"

Alistair sighed. "Go on, AllMother. No one is killing you. I need some time to think."

Thoreaux looked at the distant burning world on the screen . His body showed none of the scars or damage that had been inflicted upon it. Physically, he looked the same as he had on Pluto, the planet that was now ash.

Mentally?

He was still trying to figure out how to deal with that.

He understood what was waiting for them on the burning planet of Phoenix. For so long, he'd been molded to think strategically about how to avoid the next conflict. How to keep the AllMother alive.

He glanced away from the screen and down at his boot. Beneath the fabric was his foot, part flesh and part machine. Many of his bones had been too damaged to repair. It had been simpler for the underworld boss to build him new ones. He'd never again be in a position for someone to torture him like that. He'd die first.

Faitrin entered the room they now shared. He didn't turn around but stared at the burning planet.

"You okay, Thor?" she asked. It was her pet name for him.

He ignored the question and asked his own. "Has Pro said what he's going to do yet?"

She walked up behind him and wrapped her arms around his waist, resting her head against his back. "Not yet. He called a meeting in an hour. That's what I came to tell you. How are you feeling?"

Thoreaux put his hands on her arms. "He's going to fight."

"You sure?"

Thoreaux chuckled. "Pro doesn't know anything else to do but fight. It's what he was born to do."

"What are *you* thinking about?" Faitrin pressed.

"You don't want to know."

"I don't think that's true," Faitrin responded with her head still resting against his back. "See, when I ask something, that means I *do* want to know. It's usually how these things go."

Thoreaux wasn't sure how open he should be with her. He wasn't sure how open he should be with anyone regarding his thoughts. He'd changed, and while he understood it, he wasn't sure what others would think. "I'm just wondering how we're going to get away from this planet and where we're going to go."

Faitrin was quiet for a moment. "I don't believe you, but I'm not going to push it. When you're ready to talk, I'm here, okay?"

He turned his back on the burning world and wrapped her in his arms. He didn't say anything, only held her there. They would need to meet with Prometheus soon.

Soon, they would need to fight for their lives once again.

Thoreaux was looking forward to it.

Thoreaux had only witnessed what Prometheus did on replay. He'd been floating above the melee, mostly unconscious. He hadn't been mentally aware enough to understand what was happening, but he'd watched it on security camera footage once he healed. He'd never seen anything like it in his life. They were all lucky that Prometheus hadn't killed every one of them with his furious power.

His council had expanded by one, and Thoreaux was just now coming to grips with what these giants meant. Faitrin had explained it to him as best she could, but it had still been awkward to watch when Thoreaux first saw Caesar.

Pro was still working on convincing the gigante that he wasn't a servant, but the beast wasn't exactly taking to it.

They had gathered in a room on the lower deck: Faitrin, Relm, Thoreaux, Servia, the AllMother, Caesar, and Prometheus. Pro hadn't yet convinced Caesar of his new station, so convincing the rest of his knights was out of the question. It would take one of their own to spread that message.

They sat at a round table and all eyes were on Prometheus. Thoreaux was to his right, and Caesar to his left. The giant didn't like leaving his side if it could be helped, Thoreaux noticed.

Thoreaux watched Pro. He saw nothing physically different about the man, but he knew what he'd witnessed on those replays. He was sitting next to the most dangerous person in the entire universe.

"Our choices aren't real choices," Prometheus began. "We can give up the AllMother, or we can fight. I think everyone at this table understands we're not going to give her up."

He met their eyes individually. Thoreaux knew no one here would give up the AllMother, except perhaps Caesar, and then only if Pro commanded it.

"So that leaves us only one choice: to fight."

Thoreaux caught Faitrin's eye quickly and gave her a wink.

"With our current trajectory, we'll land in just under two standard days, though I'm not in a rush. The planet is completely occupied by the Myrmidons. If we ask our people on the planet to rise up, they will, but the cost would be too great. If we save the AllMother and lose half our people, how is it worth it?"

He looked down at the table. Thoreaux didn't like the expression on his face. Pro knew what he was going to say next wouldn't be taken well.

"I could unleash the gigantes on them, and I think the Myrmidons might find themselves in a real match then," he continued, "but again, I have other plans for them. I don't want to lose any of them in an unnecessary fight."

Servia raised her hand off the table. "Question, Pro. How is this unnecessary?"

"I don't think it's necessary that the gigantes fight," he said without looking up. "I'm going to fight. I'm going to challenge this Myrmidon to a duel. If he wins, he can have the AllMother. If he loses, they leave the planet." He raised a hand to halt the arguments that were forming on their lips. "I know many of you are going to say, 'What if you lose, Pro?' Well, if I lose, I'm not going to be too concerned about what happens after because I'll be dead."

Thoreaux had no questions to ask because the situation's reality had suddenly grown much worse if that was possible. The only thing Thoreaux had to say was simple. "You can't."

Pro didn't have a chance to answer before the others chimed in.

Relm had leaned back in his chair. "Agreed, broth. Can't do it."

"It's not worth it," Faitrin said.

Servia and the AllMother stared at him with different expressions on their faces. The AllMother didn't appear to have heard what he'd said, while Servia shook her head with a tight grin on her lips.

"What do you mean by 'challenge this Myrmidon to a duel?'" Caesar asked.

He was the only one at the table who didn't understand the implications of the phrase. The tradition hadn't crossed to his solar system or the others he'd traveled to.

Still giving the tight grin, Servia explained, "I think it started about five hundred years ago. Or at least, *re*started. Maybe it was earlier than that, though. It's an old idea that goes back thousands and thousands of years but was mostly forgotten about until one of the Imperial Ascendants brought it back. It means that any man can challenge any man to a duel, and not to accept would be to dishonor oneself. The duel is to the death, and usually there's something major at stake. It's a truly foolish system, one that only a man could invent."

The giant's face was pensive as he thought it through. "I don't understand," he eventually said.

Thoreaux stared at Pro as he spoke. "He's using it as a way to bypass more death. By challenging this Myrmidon to a one-on-one duel, he keeps everyone else out of it. No one will die but one of them, so long as the rules are followed. If it's offered, the Myrmidon will most likely accept because to refuse would make him lose his men's esteem. I don't know if the Myrmidons consider it as important as humans from our galaxy, but if they do, everything is now in *his* hands."

"What's the problem, then?" Caesar asked.

He'd never seen a Myrmidon. He didn't realize their size, strength, speed, and technological advances. He thought Prometheus was the greatest warrior in all the universe. However, while Pro was a force to be feared, there were still those more powerful.

Prometheus stopped the arguments with a smile.

"There's no need to argue about the duel," Pro said. "I gave the Myrmidon the proposition two hours ago. He accepted. We battle when I arrive."

Ajax had received the human's proposition. He wanted to duel, and the winner would take the spoils. Ajax found the endeavor primitive, harkening back to humanity's days of honor and masculine pride. Those days had passed long ago, but the Earthborn and everyone from that star system still abided by it. Ajax knew the tradition had been brought back during a time of strife by one of the Ascendants. He'd been considered a weak leader, so he allowed anyone to challenge him to a hand-to-hand duel.

The man wasn't a great leader, but he was a superb fighter. His critics died quickly, and the idea of dueling was reborn with a vengeance.

Ajax had never seen a duel. The Superior would never think of such things within their ranks or with outsiders. Dueling someone in hand-to-hand combat was a waste of time, and the humans who interacted with the Superior knew that.

Ajax felt no particular way about the duel. It wasn't his decision to make, but the AllSeer had instructed him about what to do.

The black shadow came to him and said, "Yes, accept it.

I wish my sister would have done something like this years and years ago. It would have saved me a lot of trouble."

That had been the entire conversation because none of the Superior felt any worry about facing off with a human. Even a modified human was of little consequence to those like Ajax.

The duel would come, the Prophesied One would die, and then the AllSeer would take his sister. Their fate had nearly arrived.

CHAPTER FIVE

Alistair had permitted no one to come see him in the days it took to get to the planet Phoenix. There were no arguments to be had on the matter and nothing else that needed to be said. He had contemplated numerous other tactics to get what he wanted out of this, and every one of them would end in unmitigated disaster.

The conclusion he'd come to was that there was no other way. Even his council would have to see the truth in it. Prometheus would have to win this duel, and if he did, the path in front of them would be clear. Finally, for the first time since he had begun this endeavor, he had a chance to determine the way he would go. Before now, every choice had been made *for* him. He'd been forced into all his past decisions out of necessity.

This was the last one.

He was being forced to fight this Myrmidon, but if he won, the next choices would be his and his alone to make.

Alistair hadn't yet told his council what they would do but he had an idea, one that would bring him closer to even footing with the Commonwealth. Sometimes it was hard to keep that overall picture in his mind, the final stage of this: to destroy a monarchy.

To see Luna again.

Alistair hadn't forgotten his wife's message. The Ascendant's implied threat could bring Alistair to his knees if he let it—if he focused on it or worried about it. The threat was still there, and perhaps the Ascendant had already acted on it. Maybe his wife was dead, but to think about such things would make him lose focus in the present, and then he'd surely die.

The ship eventually made it to Phoenix. The duel would take place in three standard hours.

Alistair spoke to no one as he left the ship. The council's eyes fell on him as he walked past, but he said nothing. The gigantes all watched in reverence as he passed them.

It was comical how the shorter Terram stared at these massive new creatures. They hadn't seen such things before. Alistair hid a smile as he headed to his old room, hearing one of the Terram yelling at Servia for this intrusion. Soon they'd be relieved of the remarkable duty they'd taken on of providing a home for thousands of refugees.

At least, that was what Alistair told himself as he went to his room.

He hoped no one would come to speak to him, but he knew that was foolish.

The first visitor was Caesar. The giant had to duck as he walked through the halls. His body was large enough that he had to work not to scrape the walls with his shoulders. He looked uncomfortable as he stuck his head into Alistair's rock room.

"Master, may I speak?" he boomed in his deep voice.

Alistair was lying on the rock ledge with his hands on his stomach. "I told you not to call me Master."

"I'm sorry, Master."

It was going to be a tough habit to break.

"Go ahead," Alistair told him. "What do you want to talk about?"

"Do you want me to kill this man? Or do you want your servants to kill them all? We will do it, no problem."

Alistair closed his eyes, and a warm smile spread on his face. Caesar was an intelligent being, but he was also simple in many ways. "No, but I appreciate the offer. This is something I have to do myself."

"Okay, Master," the giant responded. "Do you want me there? I can kill him while he's focused on you."

Alistair sat up then, having not fully realized how little Caesar understood about what was to happen. He looked at the giant's square head. "No. It's very important that you understand you cannot interfere, no matter what happens. Neither you nor any of the gigantes can interfere. I only want you to be there. The rest need to remain where the Terram have them now. This duel is for me to win, and me alone, okay?"

Caesar nodded. "It will be done. May I leave now, Master?"

"Yes, and don't call me Master."

Caesar opened his mouth, most likely to say, "Sorry, master," but he caught himself. He smiled, his mouth wide with delight, then tapped his temple. "Caught myself that time."

"Good job," Alistair told him, returning his smile.

The giant left, and Alistair was alone again. He was keeping time in his head. He had about two and a half hours left. He closed his eyes and waited. Obs remained at the ledge's side, his head between his paws.

Alistair could tell that the drathe was nervous. He knew the creature wanted to be involved in the battle, but he thought he understood better than Caesar why he couldn't help. Alistair reached down and stroked the animal's fur. "I'm going to win. Maybe only me and the giant believe it, but I'm going to win, okay? Try not to worry too much."

The drathe licked his hand softly. He then placed his head back between his paws and waited with his master.

He'd expected the AllMother to come at some point, but she didn't. She understood what he was doing, and there was nothing else to be said.

Alistair was just about to start warming up when Thoreaux arrived.

"Thirty minutes left."

Alistair nodded. "Just about ready." Obs stood up, walked over to the door, and licked Thoreaux's outstretched hand.

"What are you thinking?" his second asked.

"I was thinking about my wife," Alistair said as he sat up. "Wondering what she's doing right now."

"Not about the duel?"

Alistair shook his head. "No. I've killed Myrmidons before. I'll kill this one."

Thoreaux swallowed. He looked like he had something to say but wasn't sure how to say it.

"Spit it out," Alistair told him.

"You haven't seen him yet, have you? The one you're facing?"

Alistair was reaching to grab his boot when he heard the question. He looked up. "No. Why?"

Thoreaux sighed. "Well, I suppose it's nothing. No reason to discuss it now if you're not worried."

Alistair stared at him for another second with his eyebrow raised. "You sure?"

"I mean, you'll see soon enough. Nothing I say now is going to matter. I figured you might be warming up and decided to see if I could help."

Alistair grabbed his boot and started strapping it on. "Sure."

The room was too small for any kind of real practice, so the three of them headed to where the duel would take place. The Terram had a relatively small stadium that they'd built beneath the ground. There was only one on the entire planet, given the restrictions placed on such endeavors. The stadium could hold a few hundred Terram, and usually some sort of sporting event was held in it. Not a blood sport, though.

As the three of them stepped into the stadium, Alistair stopped. He had honestly not considered the duel very much since making his decision, and he certainly hadn't considered that there would be spectators.

Here they were, though. He'd thought the area could hold a few hundred, but as he looked around the arena, his mind told him he was staring at a thousand people. The Terram were sitting on top of each other, women in men's laps, brothers and sisters sharing seats. They were shoved in tightly up to the ceiling.

"I wasn't sure you wanted to know," Thoreaux said once he understood Alistair's shock. "They started piling in the moment we landed. First come, first served type of thing. They refused any seats to our people. They want to watch this."

Alistair turned in a circle as he looked at the spectators. "I don't understand. Why?"

Thoreaux was staring at the packed seats as he spoke. "Your legend is growing, Pro. The things you've done are spreading across this galaxy. Even the Terram are starting to respect you. The tongue-lashing Servia received was nothing like it would have been six months ago." He dropped his eyes to Alistair. "One of the Terram even asked Relm if he could get your autograph."

He raised an eyebrow. "You're kidding?"

Thoreaux shrugged. "That's what he said. So don't lose this battle because we could probably start selling your signature."

Alistair shook his head. "Come. Help me get warmed up."

The two started with some hand-to-hand fighting stances. Thoreaux was woefully overmatched, but he did his best to keep up, helping Alistair work up a light sweat. It was the first time in a while that Alistair had been able to warm up before fighting, and it felt good.

Fifteen minutes passed, and silence spread across the stadium.

Thoreaux stopped attacking and looked at the other side. The Myrmidon had entered the stadium. He was alone, staring across the field of battle from behind a black and dark-green helmet. The AllSeer's eye was scratched across the metal plate on his chest. In each hand he held a small black pole, so Alistair knew he would wield dual sabers.

He had never seen anyone try such a thing. It could be very unwieldy or very dangerous.

"Thanks, Thoreaux," Alistair said as he stared at the black figure. "I'll see you in a bit."

Thoreaux grabbed his shoulder. "*Ave*, Prometheus." His second in command left the battlefield.

Alistair squatted and touched the floor. It was dusty with the rock this stadium had been carved from. He swept some away from in front of him. He wore no armor and no shields. He was dressed in simple garments: pants and a shirt with the sleeves cut off, allowing for better movement of his arms. A light sweat had risen across his body, and his muscles felt good.

He pulled the knife from his belt and looked down at his arm.

"I do not kill for glory," he whispered to the dusty floor. The stadium's noise level started to pick up at the movement of his blade. He ignored it. "I do not kill for malice. I kill because it is right. Because if I do not kill, those who seek to harm me and those I love will do so."

He brought the blade to his left arm and started cutting in a circle. The crowd above him screamed—whether cheering or booing, Prometheus did not care. The man who loved his wife, the one who cared about the AllMother's movement and her children, was gone, forced to the back of the shared mind.

Prometheus, the harbinger of fire, had arrived.

"I do not fear the enemy. I do not fear death. I only fear

living without protecting those I love. I only fear cowardice and hiding from my duty. As this blood flows, so will I. I bleed now so that I will not later. I bleed now so that those who sow harm against me know that blood does not frighten me. I bleed now because it is this blood that will conquer anyone in my path."

He looked up and across the stadium.

"See it and fear," he whispered. "See it and die."

He stood, sheathing his blade, then wiped his blood beneath his eyes. The crowd was roaring so loudly that Prometheus could feel the vibrations on his flesh.

The Myrmidon pumped his blades up and down, and green lasers spilled out on both sides.

Alistair took his Whip from his belt. The two were maybe a hundred yards from one another. Alistair couldn't see the Myrmidon's face, and he could not judge his size. He was larger than any Myrmidon Prometheus had faced before. He might have been as large as a gigante. It would be close without a doubt.

Gigantes couldn't wield dual lasers, though.

Prometheus' Whip twirled at his side, and he started forward. The Myrmidon didn't move, remaining in place holding his dual blades.

Halfway across, Prometheus picked up his pace to a jog. Fifty yards left.

At twenty-five yards, he hit an all-out sprint. His feet touched the ground only long enough to push him forward, his long steps gracefully moving him toward the beast.

The Myrmidon didn't move.

Prometheus hit the ground one last time, then threw

himself into the air on an arc toward the creature. His Whip formed a blade, the point heading toward the Myrmidon's heart.

Seconds before Prometheus made contact, the Myrmidon disappeared. He was simply no longer in front of Prometheus. The warrior tucked and rolled. He skidded to a stop, feeling the air moving behind him. Remaining low, he turned and swept his Whip through the space.

The Myrmidon was there, a towering figure. His dual blades flashed down, slashing at Prometheus and the Whip simultaneously. Prometheus didn't have time to consider what had happened and how the Myrmidon had transferred from one space to another without being seen.

The onslaught was incredible.

Prometheus rolled away, then his massive body sprang up. He had to spin again to create more space because the Myrmidon was just *there,* all over him, no matter how far Prometheus tried to push away.

The dual blades came down again and again, the creature swinging them not tiring. Prometheus used his Whip as quickly as he could, batting away the deathblows that fell on him, but he couldn't find a way inside the Myrmidon's strikes.

The right blade sliced through the air as an uppercut, catching Prometheus' ribcage and burning through garment and flesh alike. The spectators roared at the hit.

Prometheus kicked out, hit the Myrmidon in his chest, and launched himself backward at the same time, finally creating needed space between the two of them.

His ribcage burned, and he touched it with his free hand. The bone was still intact. The laser had only grazed him. The Myrmidon stood a few yards away, chuckling beneath his helmet. "You're the Prophesied One? The man that is supposed to bring the AllMother an empire?"

Prometheus said nothing. He forced the pain from his mind and started forward again. He didn't understand how anyone could move as this creature did, seeming to be everywhere at once and even able to teleport.

That wasn't possible, yet Prometheus could see no other way the being had moved as he had.

Prometheus' Whip connected with the dual blades, but he didn't force anything. His body reacted to the other's attacks, but his mind had switched to observation mode. He watched as the Myrmidon fought, trying to understand what exactly was happening.

It was hard to see the beast moving, his speed was that great. The dual blades appeared to be at one place one moment, yet the very next, they moved somewhere else. Prometheus could barely keep up, and his mind was observing. Instead of reacting, he was losing his ability to counter the attacks.

Another blade sliced deep into his left arm, almost touching bone. Pro made no noise. He spun back, his Whip arcing outward and reestablishing much-needed space between him and the Myrmidon. Blood dripped down his left arm, down his hand, and hit the ground.

"Lay down your Whip, Prophesied One," the Myrmidon commanded, "and I will make your death quick."

The crowd around them had grown quiet. Prometheus had two wounds now, and his clothing was growing dark with blood. Even if he managed to keep fighting, the blood loss would accumulate. The crowd knew he was in a bad spot. Soon he'd grow woozy, then the Myrmidon would deliver the killing blow.

He fights differently than the gigantes, Pro thought as he stared at the armored creature. *There's no rage or strength. He's all speed and calm. He fights like me.*

"You can't kill me," the Myrmidon said. "You're only human."

Prometheus watched as the creature suddenly flashed ten yards to his right. He didn't walk there, just appeared. As quickly as he'd done that, he flashed back to his original spot.

He was teleporting, or the closest thing to it Prometheus had ever seen. Magic, or science he didn't understand? It came down to the same thing right now.

Even the small murmurs in the crowd had ceased. They'd seen it too.

Luna's voice spoke to Pro. *Did you come here to die, Allie? Or to admire this Myrmidon? Because it doesn't seem like you came here to win.*

Prometheus' chest heaved as the Myrmidon remained in one place. He was silent, his blades hanging like death at his sides.

Prometheus dropped to one knee, his Whip twirling in the air at his side. He reached into the dust and lightly rubbed his fingers through it. Something was happening here that he didn't understand, something driving the very essence of this battle. It wasn't magic but some sort of technology the AllSeer had created.

Or adapted.

The Myrmidon remained still, staring through his helmet, waiting for Prometheus' next strike.

Pro finally thought he understood what was happening. He didn't know *how* it was possible, only that he saw no other way for the creature to move in such a manner. He scooped up a bit of dust in his hand, and still kneeling on one knee, tossed it to the left. He watched the dust cloud float as blood leaked from his arm.

Prometheus stood. He felt himself weakening. Not quickly, not yet; his body was far too strong for that, but any more wounds, and he'd start going faster. His eyes narrowed as he stared at the Myrmidon. He didn't know *what* the creature was. Certainly not human, but he thought he understood it now.

For the first time, the Myrmidon came at him. Pro watched his steps. They were slow and steady, nothing like the speed that he'd seen or the teleportation he'd showcased. Right now, he moved like a human. But in a few seconds?

Prometheus closed his eyes as the creature came for him. He understood what had to be done, and knew he probably only had one opportunity to do it. Once the Myrmidon understood that *he* understood, things would change quickly and for the worse.

The crowd above was silent. Prometheus felt the tiny vibrations made by the Myrmidon's movement. He could feel the dual sabers spinning as the Myrmidon set up for the killing blow.

Prometheus took a deep breath, and for milliseconds, all the minor vibrations stopped.

Pro spun with all the speed and strength he could muster, and an audible gasp ripped from the crowd's collective lungs. The Whip turned blade-like and

Prometheus thrust it forward, eyes still closed, trusting his other senses rather than sight.

He felt the laser hit home, sinking through metal armor and piercing something softer. Prometheus had been facing the opposite way as he thrust his Whip, but now he turned his head and opened his eyes. The Myrmidon stood in front of him, the blades at his side and shaking rapidly. Pro gripped the Whip's hilt with both hands and shoved it deeper, forcing it all the way through the creature until the laser exited his back.

That black blood Prometheus had seen on the Myrmidon's ship—the blood that had sprung *from* the ship—now fell from underneath the Myrmidon's helmet.

It hit his chest and the ground, steaming into the cool air.

Prometheus took his left hand off the hilt and flipped the Myrmidon's helmet to the ground.

Black blood poured from the creature's mouth. The thing Pro was looking at was ancient. Not old in the sense of the AllMother, but old in the sense of something long ago dead. Its skin was black and a deep green like the armor he'd worn, but sickly-looking, like it was rotting. Something moved beneath his flesh as well, looking like tiny ants crawling underneath his skin.

The dual blades dropped to the ground.

Prometheus grabbed the hilt again and shoved, this time putting the Myrmidon on the floor. He pulled the Whip upward, cutting farther into the creature's chest cavity. That oil-like blood flowed from his mouth. The creature's eyes were red and stared up at Prometheus in disbelief, with complete and total shock that he'd been beaten.

The insects beneath his skin were slowing, if that was what they were. Prometheus didn't know, and he didn't care. He only wanted this thing *dead*.

He wrenched the Whip farther up, ripping through the chest and then splitting the creature's neck and head wide open, obliterating the thing's face.

The screaming above Prometheus was deafening. The very walls of the place were vibrating with cheers.

Prometheus stood straight up, pulling his Whip from the dead Myrmidon, and looked across the throng of people. On the other side of the stadium, he saw Thoreaux and Servia standing side by side. They were smiling.

Alistair slowly started coming forward, the blood-lusting Prometheus stepping back. As he did, he felt the weakness in his body, the blood still flowing from his arm.

He took a step forward and wobbled on his feet.

There was more to the damage than blood loss. He knew that now. Those blades... Something had been in the lasers, and now it was in Alistair. He dropped to his knees, and the last thing he remembered was Servia and Thoreaux rushing toward him.

Blackness embraced him.

CHAPTER SIX

Alistair dreamed.

They weren't like most of his dreams, the dreams of the modified, but they were still very strange.

He stood next to the Imperial Ascendant, Alexander de Finita. He'd met the man before, although until Alistair's transformation, he doubted Alexander would have remembered him.

Now, he stood inside a place he'd never been. The Imperial Ascendant was slightly in front of him and to the side. A relatively large orb floated in front of the Ascendant, with a light circle around it. The Ascendant appeared to be speaking, but Alistair couldn't hear him.

He looked around the room, seeing the royal purple of the Ascendancy on the walls. Other than that, this room was bare, other than the orb in the middle.

This isn't real, he told himself, yet he didn't fully believe it.

The dreams of the modified. They were something he'd

never asked about, not even during all those times he'd seen his wife in them.

Alistair walked up to the orb, and the light flashed to a single dot. It looked like an eye's pupil, and it moved across the orb's surface until it was staring at him.

"So, it's happened?"

To Alistair, it sounded like multiple voices were saying the same words in unison. He instinctively took a step back, not understanding what was happening or how it could see him.

"If you come," the orb said, "we will kill all that you love. Those who serve next to you will die. Your wife will die. Everything you hold dear will cease to exist, and we will make you watch it all happen. You must understand that before you continue this crusade. We may lose, but we will burn you to the ground in the process."

Alistair had no idea who or what he was hearing. He turned to look at the Ascendant, but the man was staring at the orb with bewilderment on his face.

He turned back to the orb. The single dot was still staring at him.

"Do not return, Alistair Kane. Remain at peace where you are now or travel elsewhere. We don't care. Just do not return to Earth. Not if you care about those who serve you and those who love you."

Alistair blinked, expecting to see the orb in front of him again. It was gone, and so was the simple room with its royal purple decor. Alistair started to look at his new surroundings but stopped when he saw his wife. She was sitting at a window, staring out of it with tears in her eyes. It was obvious some had already fallen. Her face was on the verge of puffiness, and her eyes were red. She wasn't trembling, although her hands were clenched on her lap.

Alistair crossed the small room with giant steps and had nearly reached his wife when he stopped.

She turned to look over her shoulder. Surprise bordering on shock covered her face.

She heard me, he thought. *Or something very close to it.*

He didn't move, and she didn't turn away. The tears in her eyes were on the verge of falling, but she no longer looked sad. Luna looked frightened.

"Is someone there?" she asked, her voice shaking.

Slowly, Alistair sank to his knees so that he was at eye level with his wife. Her eyes darted around the room in fear.

"It's me, love," he whispered.

Luna's eyes grew wider. "Who's there?"

"Allie. It's me—Allie," he answered, tears in his own eyes now. What was happening, where he was—those things had ceased to matter. He was in front of his wife for the first time in long months, and somehow she could sense him.

His wife stood then, her hands trembling. She shook her head as if trying to clear something out.

Alistair was staring up at her, about to say something else, but the room around him started to fade. "*NO!*" he shouted, "I don't want to leave!"

He stood and reached for his wife, wanting to hold her despite the fear stamped on her face. Everything was fading, though, the vibrant colors turning black.

As he wrapped his arms around her, there was nothing left to see—only darkness.

Luna felt her heart thudding in her chest. She heard it in her ears and felt sweat popping out across her forehead, even as goosebumps rose on her arms.

Seconds passed, each one feeling like an eternity.

Luna's breath was caught in her throat, her lungs still. She didn't force herself to breathe but stared into the space before her.

Had she heard *his* voice?

Had she heard Alistair?

It's me—Allie.

Whispers, if they could be called that. Luna wasn't sure she'd heard anything, yet those three words kept ringing through her head.

It's me—Allie.

Luna let the air exit her lungs. Her hands were shaking, and she folded them in her lap again.

She'd been having those weird dreams ever since she was told he'd died. Alistair was always in the dreams, and they were unlike anything she'd ever experienced. The two of them were often in the past, but each of them did things slightly differently from how they had actually happened.

Luna didn't know what they'd meant, if anything.

But this?

Someone—or something—had been in the room with her. She'd felt their presence as if it had been a physical body right next to her.

Tears flooded Luna's eyes. She brought her shaking hands to her face and started weeping. Her shoulders heaved.

It had felt like Alistair. It had felt like her husband.

But that wasn't possible, and Luna knew it. She understood that her mind was creating phantoms because of how much she missed him.

Her life was frightening, and the only person who could bring her any solace was her husband. He wasn't here, though. He couldn't be here, no matter how much she wanted it to be so.

Luna cried alone in her room inside the Imperial Residence. Later that day, she would meet with the Imperial Ascendant. He'd know she'd been crying.

Even with that in the back of her mind, she couldn't stop.

She missed her husband and knowing that he was out there without her...

It broke Luna's heart.

Alistair opened his eyes, panic gripping him. He surged upward and found strong hands holding him back. Alistair struggled, his hand throttling outward for purchase on whoever held him down.

"Pro, calm down!"

He held someone's neck in his hand, panic and rage possessing him.

"PRO!"

It was Thoreaux's voice, and it finally shoved through the shock of being next to his wife and then losing her. Alistair saw the room in front of him. The strong hands were Caesar's. He held the giant's neck, and there was a look of shock on the giant's face.

Alistair released him and fell back on the cot.

Thoreaux stood on one side, Caesar on the other.

"What happened?" Alistair asked.

"You got a little banged up in the battle," Thoreaux said, "but you're stable now."

Caesar's huge hands still held Alistair's shoulder, though the strength in them had lessened.

"How long have I been out?" Alistair asked.

He saw Thoreaux's lips draw into a line for a moment. "Two weeks. It got pretty close there for a while."

Alistair blinked in disbelief. "Two weeks? What about the Myrmidons? Where are they?"

"After you killed the one, they were as good as their word. They packed up and left. So long as we're here on this planet, they're not going to attempt anything. The one you chopped up…" Thoreaux shook his head and looked at Caesar.

The giant's hand now rested on Alistair's shoulders. "He was not human, not gigante either. He was something else."

Thoreaux nodded and found Alistair again. "We did an inspection of his remains. It was pretty interesting stuff, Pro. As far as I know, that's the first Myrmidon we've ever been able to look at. Those guys have biological material in them, but they've got a lot of non-biological stuff, too." He paused for a second. "How did you realize what he was or what he was going to do?"

Alistair was lying back on the cot. It was hard for him to forget what he'd just seen, that floating orb and his wife and the *realness* he'd felt. As if he'd actually been there, across galaxies, with the Imperial Ascendant and Luna. The two standing next to him had no idea about it, though. They were asking him questions about the fight. To Alistair, that was the furthest thing from his mind.

"Where's the AllMother?" he asked, ignoring their question.

"I'm not sure," Thoreaux answered. "The Terram said they could safely wake you up, so we wanted to be here when they did."

Alistair closed his eyes. "Bring her to me."

"Right now?" Thoreaux asked.

He nodded. "Yeah. I need to talk to her. Just her, though. Everyone else can wait."

"Okay, Pro. We'll go get her."

Alistair could hear the skepticism in Thoreaux's voice, but he didn't care at the moment. He didn't care about the soreness in his body, or what the Myrmidon had done to him. There'd be time for that later. Right now, he needed to know if what he'd seen had been real and how it was possible.

Minutes passed, as did the adrenaline coursing through Alistair's veins. He looked around the room while he waited. The Terram had a lot of medical equipment in here, which contrasted awkwardly with the prehistoric-looking red stone walls they'd carved their habitations out of. Alistair didn't know what he was looking at, but he guessed it was what had kept him alive.

Eventually, the old woman walked in. She paused at the door, crossing her arms over her stomach. "That was the first time I've ever been worried about you. I didn't know what they were made of or I would have said something.

They aren't all like that one. The ones I killed on Pluto certainly weren't. He was different. Maybe special to my brother."

"I don't care about that right now. I need you to listen and tell me what's happening," he said as he turned his head to look at her. "Come closer. I don't want anyone else hearing this."

The AllMother did as he instructed, her arms still folded over her body. She looked tired and worn out. This was taking its toll on her; Alistair could see that. Perhaps his injury had scared her. Even so, he didn't truly care at that moment. He couldn't quit thinking about his wife, and that was all-consuming.

"You know about the dreams, I take it?" he asked. "Being modified yourself and all."

The old woman nodded.

Alistair told her what he'd seen. He told her about all the dreams from when they'd first begun to this last one.

When he finished, he looked at her. "I want to know what it means. I want to know if it's real."

The AllMother glanced away from him at the room's equipment. A lot of it was technology they didn't have on Earth. Some of the floating screens were visible. She walked over to one on the right and touched the side of it. It was not only a digital creation but physical as well. "I don't understand how this works, Alistair," she said. "I know that it does work, that it helped save your life, but I can't tell how. *You* are becoming like that to me. I know you can do things I could only dream of, but not how."

"What are you saying?" he asked. "Those are just words. I need you to be specific. Are the things I'm seeing real?"

"I can't say for certain, Alistair," she told him as she turned from the hanging screen. "I'll tell you what I think. You're evolving beyond anything I imagined. I think the first dreams you had were shared dreams. I imagine your wife had some of the same dreams. Your mind allowed you both to experience them. That's..."

Her voice trailed off as she walked over to one of the ledges built into the wall and took a seat.

"That in itself is new to me. When they talk about the dreams of the modified, the consensus is that sometimes the physically modified get a glimpse of things that happened in the past, or maybe in the future. I always believed it was a glitch from what my father did to us. Some kind of hangover in the system where the physically modified got a bit of my modification. My dreams were deeper than that, but I never *shared* a dream with anyone." She met his eyes. "I think what you did before you woke up is very, very different from anything I've heard of."

"So I was there? In the room with my wife?"

"I..." She paused for a second as if trying to find the words. "I don't *know*, Alistair. You are advancing far beyond anything I thought possible. The tech I used for you wasn't the same as my father's, and I spent years trying to expand it, to perfect it. Trying to make sure you'd have the best chance. None of the modifications were meant to produce anything like you're describing, though. You're venturing out beyond the original specifications."

Alistair leaned his head back on the cot. "'Specifications?'" It sounded like he was some kind of tool. "What does it mean?"

"It means you're going to be greater than I ever imagined," she said. "It means your powers are going to increase. I honestly can't say how far they'll stretch."

"I'm not in control of any of it," Alistair said. "Outside of my physical body, these modifications are doing as they please. I don't know how to control it. It's controlling *me*."

The AllMother was quiet for a few seconds before asking, "Has the modification done anything bad to you? Has it hurt you or manipulated you in some way that hasn't been helpful, or at least neutral?"

Alistair thought about the dreams that he'd apparently shared with his wife. Somehow their two minds had found a common place to meet. There hadn't been anything negative in the dreams. In fact, most of them had been enjoyable. Even this last one, where he saw that orb and then his wife, hadn't been negative, just shocking.

"They're either neutral or helpful," he responded after a few moments.

The AllMother nodded. "Perhaps you can't control them yet, or maybe you won't ever be able to, I honestly can't say. If they aren't doing anything to harm you, then I wouldn't worry about them too much."

"Do you know what that orb was?" Alistair asked. "The one with the light on its exterior?"

The AllMother once again grew quiet and looked at the technology floating through the room. "I've never heard of that before, but it concerns me. You said it sounded like many voices were speaking as one?"

Alistair nodded.

"But it didn't say who they were?"

"No, just that they would kill everyone I loved. They, or it, would kill you, the movement, Luna. Everyone."

The AllMother let out a long sigh. "The modification showed you something that you needed to see. At least, that's what I think is happening. I don't know what that orb is, but if the Ascendant was there, then it's important. You'll need to find that out, Prometheus, as we go forward. I think that's what it was showing you. There's more to this than I understand."

Alistair closed his eyes. He could still see his wife's fearful face, wondering who was in the room with her. He couldn't focus on her right now. There was much to do, and he had to understand what state his body was in. "Thank you. Would you send Thoreaux back in?"

"As you wish." The old woman stood and walked to Alistair's cot. She placed her hand on his shoulder, perhaps the first time the two had touched. "You scared me, but I'm glad you pulled through. I didn't realize how much I needed you, Alistair."

It was an odd moment of vulnerability from the woman who had kept much of her life a secret, someone who had purposefully built a group of people who saw her as a demi-god, now showing Alistair her vulnerability. More, it was working on her physically as well. Seeing him unconscious for two weeks on this cot had drained her.

"I'm here, AllMother," he replied. "I'm back. Send me Thoreaux. There's still a lot to do."

She nodded and left the room. A couple of minutes later, Thoreaux came back in with Caesar.

"Okay," Alistair started. "Tell me what I missed."

Thoreaux went into detail about the things they'd discovered with the Myrmidon. He was a hybrid creature. There was biology in him, but there were mechanical pieces that Thoreaux couldn't understand. The Terram were still conducting tests on the corpse, but it was disintegrating rather quickly. The mechanical pieces had been some kind of nanotechnology that allowed him to flow from one place to another without the human eye detecting it. Thoreaux threw up some cameras so Alistair could watch the Myrmidon with things slowed down by a factor of ten.

Sure enough, the creature hadn't been teleporting but breaking apart into nearly infinite pieces. The armor he wore had just been another part of him or part of the technology that made him. From the video alone, Alistair couldn't be sure. "He's dead? You're confident of it?"

"As dead as something like that can be, I suppose. His biological material is deteriorating more quickly than it should. The Terram are trying to freeze it for research, but it seems like the AllSeer ensured that wouldn't be possible. How did you know what to do when you were fighting him, Pro?"

Alistair shook his head. "I'm not entirely sure. I just knew he was too fast, and I had to attack where he would be, not where he was. I guess I caught him when he was reassimilating or whatever you'd call it. I figured I had one chance because once he knew that I knew what was happening, he'd use another tactic. I didn't want to risk that. His lasers, they did something besides cut me?"

"Yeah, there was poison in them, Pro, but not like the kind you're thinking. That nanotechnology that helped make up the Myrmidon also made up his weapons. When he cut you, those nanocytes or whatever you want to call them entered your body and started attacking your organs. Sort of the opposite of what Caesar does."

The giant was standing at the doorway, his hand at his sides.

"It was close, Pro," Thoreaux continued. "That nanotech is a bitch, and no one was equipped to deal with it. The Terram and Caesar helped you pull through."

"How well am I?" he asked. "Am I able to continue?"

"Yeah," Thoreaux answered. "You may be a little weaker for a bit, but the nanotech is out of your bloodstream. You're just getting back up to full speed now."

"I'm going to owe my entire life to the Terram," Alistair mused. "Okay, update me on where we are strategically. I'm ready to get all of us off this planet. Our whole group, not just the council. The Terram have done enough for us."

"Well, Pro, that's sorta the thing. The Terram have..."

Thoreaux looked at Caesar, trying to find the words.

Caesar supplied, "They are your servants too."

Alistair sat up on the cot and spun his legs so they hung off the side. Thoreaux was chuckling. "Not quite, but close. Caesar still thinks we're all your servants, although I've been working diligently on that. The Terram are pledging loyalty to you, Pro. Their political structures are somewhat foreign to us, having both a king and democratic voting body of senators, but both groups pledged fealty to you. The Terram are now your vassals."

Alistair didn't understand. "Slow down. What are you saying?"

"You have your knights, Pro." Thoreaux flicked his hand toward Caesar. "You're getting your true army now. They saw what you could do—what you did—to the Myrmidon. In this galaxy, and in others, I imagine, the Myrmidons have come and gone with impunity. No one could stop them; no one even dared. You just killed one of the top Myrmidons in the universe, then survived technology meant to poison you. The Terram see that power, and they don't want to end up on the wrong side of it."

He put both hands on Alistair's shoulders.

"It's a miracle, what you've done. Beyond genius. An entire planet has pledged loyalty to you and will do what you want, Pro. We have ships now. If we want to tax them, gods, we could do that too. Do you understand?"

Alistair stared at his lap. This wasn't what he'd wanted at all. He wanted to find his wife, not have vassals and people pledging fealty to him.

"Before you start getting upset that things have changed, you need to think this through, Pro." Thoreaux removed his hands from Alistair's shoulders. "The goal hasn't changed. Death to the Ascendancy. Even with our knights, we're not strong enough to go there. We're not strong enough to face the AllSeer either. You can't challenge every single one of them to a duel until they're all dead. We will *have* to find vassals. More of them. Perhaps many more. This is the first. If you ask me, it's sent from the gods themselves."

A lot had happened while Alistair was unconscious. He was being told a lot of things at once, and his original plans seemed like something he'd thought up in another lifetime in the light of what he had learned. Yet, listening to Thoreaux, he thought the man was right.

"Let me ask then, they'll give us ships?"

"Pretty much anything you ask. It's good to remember history, and an overbearing monarch always risks a revolt. But within reason, they're going to let you have it."

Alistair started to stand, and his legs immediately felt shaky.

"Sit down, Pro," Thoreaux instructed. "What do you need?"

"I need an AI."

"I'm here," came the English accented response from Jeeves. "How can I help?"

A diagram floated through the air until it was on Alistair's left, allowing all three individuals to look at it. It showed was a man dressed in an ancient-looking suit with a monocle in one eye.

"I know you bio-creatures like to think of things in terms of male and female, so I designed this chap while you were dozing, Pro." The little character on the floating screen spoke, but it was the AI's voice everyone heard. "What is it that you need?"

"The gigantes," Alistair began. "Do you know where they're bred? What planet their corporation holds this school on, and how far away it is?"

"Of course, I do," the character said with a grin.

Alistair raised his eyebrows. "Well, would you mind telling me?"

"Of course, I was just waiting for you to ask. The planet is roughly a two-month-long flight."

Thoreaux turned away from the AI's image. "What do you have in mind?"

"I'm curious to know this as well," Caesar said.

"We're going to that planet, and I'm going to free any

gigantes. After, those that want to join up with me are welcome, but all are free to do what they want, so long as it isn't continuing to enslave one another."

Thoreaux opened his mouth as if to speak, but no words came out. He looked at Caesar, whose mouth was also agape. The giant was staring at Alistair with unadulterated disbelief. "Master," he finally whispered. "That isn't possible. That cannot be done. It is not the way of things. It goes against *nature*."

Alistair didn't look up as the gigante spoke but kept staring at his lap. This was why he hadn't involved the giants in his fight against the Myrmidon. He understood they would be needed later and for something perhaps even more important. "This is what I want, Caesar, and it's what we're going to do. If you have objections or do not want to participate, I understand. You're a free being and can do as you choose, but I'm going to that planet and I'm going to free all those like you. No one will be sold into slavery when I'm finished. Never again."

Caesar was silent. Thoreaux's eyes went from the giant to his leader. "You're serious?" he finally asked.

Alistair looked up. "I'm dead serious. That's where I'm going next. You with me?"

Thoreaux shrugged and looked down at his shoes, grinning. "There are worse things to do than freeing people. I hope the rest of these giants don't smell as bad as Caesar, though, for all of our sakes."

Caesar looked shocked, but Thoreaux glanced up and winked. "Just kidding, big man." He turned to Alistair. "I follow you to the end. You know that. If you say we go free the giants, then we go free the giants."

"And you, Caesar? Are you with me?"

"I'll do whatever you say, Master," the giant responded. Alistair thought he saw something resembling fear on his face, maybe for the first time. Not quite the same as fear, but close—a cousin of it, perhaps. "This is not like before. This is not like the crime lord. My home is a cold place, one that does not allow life to live unless it is strong. Many will die, Master. Many of those you love. It is important to me that you understand this. Those who bred me will do anything to keep what they have. And my kind? They know nothing but to defend that way of life. I will do as you wish, Master, but we will not survive this."

Alistair stood up very carefully, using the giant's massive arm to steady himself. As he stood, he realized how much weight he'd lost since being unconscious. He needed nutrition and exercise, but he'd get those things on their way to this new planet.

He looked the giant in the eyes. "Leave how we survive to me, Caesar. So long as you're with me, that's all I need to know."

"I'm with you, Master," the giant said.

CHAPTER SEVEN

Alistair spent the first month of the voyage training. He took it seriously and even asked Linc to travel aboard his dreadnought.

It felt like ages since the two of them had last worked together. When Alistair first started training again, his body was weak and underweight. Within two weeks, he'd regained most of his weight and all of his strength.

He and Linc trained in the dreadnought's war room, and now it was Linc who was on the losing sides of the encounters.

Picking himself up off the floor after their last session, Linc remained on a knee and looked at Alistair. "It's true what they say? Your mind is like the AllMother's?"

Alistair pulled his shirt off, sweat covering his ripped torso. His hulking back was to Linc, and he was quiet while he used his shirt to dry himself.

Linc continued, "I heard that something happened on the planet you were on. I heard it was something pretty outrageous, Pro. Something only the AllMother could have done, and maybe not even her. Is it true?"

Alistair let his shirt drop to his side. He looked down at the floor. "Something happened, yes, but I'm not like the AllMother. She can control her mind, but I..." He turned so that the two faced each other. "I'm not sure I can. Why are you asking, Linc? Are others commenting on it?"

Linc placed his pole across his lap, rubbing one side with his right hand. "I can't say if people are talking about it or not. I stay away from the gossip." He turned his head to the left. "Oh, there he is."

Obs had poked his head into the war room. He saw Linc and immediately padded over to his old owner. Linc scratched behind the drathe's ears while Obs sat down on his hind legs. Linc looked up at Alistair. "I'd also heard that you weren't able to control it like the AllMother."

Alistair raised an eyebrow. "I thought you stayed away from gossip? You're hearing an awful lot for staying so far away from it."

Linc raised a hand in protest. "Woah, woah. I didn't say I stayed far away from it, only that I stayed away. Sometimes it follows me, though."

He stood up, putting one end of his pole on the ground and leaning on it. Obs walked over to his master. "I ask because I might be able to help some with the controlling part. Not a lot. I truly don't understand it, but I understand the mind-body connection well. If you're ever interested, we could sit down and talk about it. See where we can go."

Alistair nodded. He wasn't sure how much he wanted to involve anyone in this, mainly because *he* didn't want to be involved with it; he just had no choice. "I'll keep that in mind, Linc."

The trainer nodded and picked up his pole. "I was wrong about you combining the forms, Pro. I honestly didn't think it was possible, but the things you're able to do now surpass anything I've ever seen. I just wanted you to know that I recognize I was wrong."

Alistair nodded. He squatted down and started petting the drathe. "Thanks, Linc. Would you do me a favor? Would you send Caesar in here?"

"No problem, Pro," the trainer said.

Alistair sat down on the floor as Linc left. The drathe sat in front of him, master and subject looking into one another's eyes. "You think Linc can help me figure out my crazy mind?" Alistair asked.

Obs looked out the door from which Linc had left. He stared for a few seconds, then gave a small bark.

"Is that a maybe?"

Obs shoved his big head past Alistair's hands and nuzzled his chin with his snout.

Alistair laughed. "You're a good dog."

The drathe bit his ear lightly in protest.

"Master?" The voice boomed from the door. "You called me?"

Remaining seated, Alistair turned as Obs flopped into his lap, almost causing him to fall over. "Goodness." Alistair shook his head. "He thinks he's a lap drathe or something." He focused his eyes on the giant while he stroked the animal's fur. "Come on in, Caesar. I wanted to talk to you some while I'm alone."

"Yes, Master," the giant responded before stepping

farther into the war room. He and Alistair hadn't practiced together yet, but Alistair thought it might be a good idea soon. The two of them had battled each other and battled together against others, but practicing would give them an edge in what would come next.

Alistair stroked the drathe some more and pointed with his left hand at the space in front of him. "Sit with me for a bit?"

The giant nodded and sat down in front of the man he considered his master. He moved fluidly for someone his size and was able to fold his legs beneath each other. "What would you like to talk about, Master?" he asked in his almost overly formal way.

"Well, I think it's time we talked about this master-servant relationship. Do you know who the first Caesar was? Well, I think he was the first. Do you know why I named you after him?"

The giant shook his head. Such things had never been important to him. He wasn't supposed to know history, not humanity's or his own. His purpose was simple: to serve those stronger than him.

It was time that changed.

"He was one of the greatest leaders that ever lived. A king-like person that conquered the known world. Caesar served no one but himself."

The giant's eyes widened. "Everyone serves someone."

"Who do I serve?"

The giant was quiet for a second and looked down at Obs. "You serve those beneath you."

"In a way, I guess I do. It's my job to ensure their safety, but if I want to stop doing that, I could. If I reach this planet and say, 'I'm finished,' no one can stop me. I can walk away at any time. Do you understand?"

Not looking up, the giant nodded.

"Then, Caesar, why can't you? What's the difference between us that says you can't walk away from something when you want to? Or any of those like you?"

The giant rubbed one of his large hands over the top of his head. His hair was long, and his head was massive and square. Alistair knew such simple questions had never been put to the gigante before.

Caesar looked up. "You," he pointed at Alistair, "are human. I'm not. I was made to serve. *Bred* to serve. You were made to lead, born from father and mother. That is the difference." He placed his hand back in his lap.

Alistair shook his head. "That's what you were told to think, but it's not true. The people who made you don't have any say over what you do, Caesar. While I respect and love my parents, they have no say over my life. They haven't since I left for the Academy. Only you get to decide your life. How you were born, or where you were born, why would that decide anything?"

"Because they said so," the giant responded, and then Alistair saw understanding in his eyes. Alistair thought the creature was realizing the illogic in the words and seeing they didn't hold up under scrutiny.

"That's right," Alistair said with a nod. "They did say so, and now I'm saying differently. I'm saying that you don't have to listen to me, or them, or anyone else. If you want, right now, you can try to kill me and my pet here."

Obs looked up with surprise on his face.

Alistair smiled and petted the drathe's head. "Of course,

I'd rather you didn't, but you get my point. You aren't my servant. Not my slave. You're a free being, a gigante. The first of your kind to be recognized as free." Alistair paused and looked down at the drathe. He knew that what he'd just told the gigante would take time to sink in, but he'd seen the knowledge in his eyes. Once an idea like that set in, it couldn't be extinguished. The next part of this was just as important as the first. Both for Caesar and himself, as well as his movement. "You can follow me or you can go your own way, Caesar. However, I don't know how many of you there are. I'm going to find out soon. I do know that every single one of them thinks as you do, or did. Every gigante that has been bred considers himself a servant or a slave."

He looked up.

"They don't have to. You can change their minds. Not just those on this ship who look at me as their master, but the ones on the planet we're soon to be at. You have an opportunity that I don't have here, Caesar. You can free your people, just as I'm attempting to free my own. I can't set all of the gigantes loose. They'll never hear me, or listen to me. I'm an outsider. More than likely, they'll only want to be enslaved by me. You, though?"

Alistair stood, moving Obs off his lap.

"You can be the leader they need. The leader who sets them all free. The leader they need."

The gigante slowly got to his feet, not taking his eyes off Alistair. "Is this a trick?"

Alistair took his right arm in his hand. "I would never trick you, Caesar. You are part of my pack now. More, what would I gain from trying it? Nothing. You're free,

Caesar. You've been free since the moment I met you, but now I'm telling you as your 'master.' You are a free being, and your choices are only yours now. I will no longer command you or accept your subservience. You follow me if you want to, Caesar."

The giant blinked a few times. There was a gleam in his eye that his facial features couldn't adequately express. Something was happening inside the big creature's head.

" I...I need to think," Caesar said. "I'm going to go now. I'm going to go think."

It was one of the happiest moments Alistair had ever experienced, and besides Obs, no one else was there to see it. The giant didn't look at Alistair for approval. He didn't ask if it was okay. He dropped his eyes to the floor, turned, and walked out of the room, obviously deep in thought.

Alistair and Obs were left alone in the war room. He looked down at the drathe. The animal was staring at him. "Two things. Every creature deserves freedom, and free beings fight harder."

Obs barked loudly.

"Oh, no," Alistair responded. "You're stuck with me forever. No freedom for you."

The drathe nipped his hand.

CHAPTER EIGHT

Caesar was large, nearly two hundred and thirty kilograms of dense muscle. His head was huge in a way not seen on humans. He moved slowly unless the situation called for him to be fast. Then there were few in the universe who could move as quickly. His size and lumbering nature made those who met him consider him a slow thinker, and combined with his somewhat stilted use of language, some might even think him dumb.

Nothing could be further from the truth. For Caesar's part, he never concerned himself with how others thought of him. His entire life had been one of brutality and brainwashing. He'd lived the early part of his life trying not to be murdered by creatures just like himself, and the second part had been spent in service to those who said his only purpose was to kill.

His mind wasn't slow, however, only abused and misled.

For the first time, Caesar was considering something new. He'd heard Prometheus tell him over and over that he wasn't a slave, but the truth of it had never settled into his mind. They were just words, without force or logic behind them.

Until today. Because for the first time, someone had given him the logic behind the words. It wasn't a treatise or proof, but something very simple.

Why did what other people say matter?

Caesar had wanted to scream, *"BECAUSE THAT'S WHAT I WAS BRED TO DO!"*

Yet, even that lacked logic. It was just emotion.

And what if it wasn't true? What if Prometheus was right? What if these people who claimed control over him had no right to do so?

Caesar made his way back to his room and almost collapsed on his bed. The walk had revealed something else that was almost paralyzing. Caesar had believed what he'd been told his whole life. He'd killed countless gigantes in his school and countless humans once out of it. He'd murdered again and again because he'd been told to.

Had all of it been due to a lie?

All of his brothers he'd murdered at school, and those he'd killed during his service to someone he'd thought his master? He didn't even bother considering the human lives he'd taken because it was humans who had *made* him do it.

How many had he killed, and how many of his brothers had murdered those like them for the same lie?

Caesar laid down in the bed and closed his eyes. He had felt this once before, the first time he killed—an infinite sadness that permeated his whole body. He felt hot tears behind his eyes, a strange thing he hadn't known since that virginal experience with murder.

The giant lay alone in his room and thought of the evil he'd done, wondering if there was time to make up for it.

For the first moment since awakening in a vat, the AllSeer was stunned.

A Superior, one from his very bloodline, had been cut down by this Prophesied One.

Millions of miles away, the AllSeer considered what it might mean.

He could not see the battle as it happened, but then, he hadn't thought it would be necessary. The Prophesied One would die, the AllMother's futile quest would end, and then the AllSeer and his sister would meet their fate together. He had watched the Prophesied One fight once before, on the AllSeer's ship, and yes, the man had been impressive.

But he was only that—a man.

A modified man, yes, but a man all the same.

Ajax had been nearly as powerful as the AllSeer. Certainly, he should have been able to kill this *human*. Ajax was no longer here, though. He'd gone to meet the gods, and the Prophesied One still lived.

The AllSeer rarely rushed to action. He'd lived long enough and seen more than enough to know that he needn't rush. His strength and power were too vast for him to move quickly.

So, back on his homeworld, he thought. He remained alone, not granting entrance to his quarters except by the slaves of whom he demanded things.

After one month, around the same time a giant was contemplating his nature in another part of the universe, the AllSeer decided what must be done.

He rose from his chair and walked out of his quarters. The slave standing outside bowed low, careful not to make eye contact. The AllSeer paid no attention but turned down the hallway. He thought about Ajax as he walked. He would not miss the man in a conventional sense, but he still found it almost inconceivable that Ajax was dead.

Perhaps something *was* different about this Prophesied One.

Perhaps his sister knew something he didn't.

These juxtaposed thoughts within his mind threatened the AllSeer for the first time in hundreds of years. His and his sister's fates were intertwined; no one could convince him otherwise. Yet, if he knew their fate and had not seen this Prophesied One enter, he was missing something very important.

The AllSeer walked outside his home and onto a world that was more technological than biological. The machinations of war had already started, and they wouldn't stop now. Above him, hanging from metal tree-like structures, were creatures waking up for the first time in centuries. The aluminum cocoons that wrapped them were peeling away, revealing the AllSeer's monstrosities.

He had thought he would have his sister by now and the assault on Earth could begin. The monsters above him couldn't be held at bay for long. They would need to feed, as most creatures did, and the AllSeer couldn't deny them that.

He walked beyond the slowly waking beings without looking at them.

To his right, a weapons plant was alive with work. Slaves were going in and out, some moving equipment containing raw materials. Again, the AllSeer ignored it all. These were things that had been started and now couldn't be stopped. The war machine would move forward, heading toward Earth, and if fate hadn't revealed itself by then, Earth and all its inhabitants would cease existing.

The AllSeer wound his way across his planet on foot, walking nine miles before finding the transport he wanted. The slave flying it said nothing as he entered the back and sat down. This transport was rarely used, and mostly by the AllSeer's scientists. He stared out the transport's windows as it rose into the air and looked down at everything he'd created. The black metal world beneath him seemed to move of its own accord, although the AllSeer knew he was the engine which moved it all.

The transport flew beyond the city and out into the burnt and blackened countryside. The AllSeer had come to this planet long ago when it was necessary to escape his father's iron fist. The planet had been green then, and an alien species that humanity had never known nor even dreamed about lived here. The AllSeer had wiped them out, every last one of them. He'd burned their green planet to ashes, and he continued to do so twice a year. If he didn't, there was a chance that life could restart on his homeworld, and it wasn't something he wished to ever see again.

The transport finally reached the place that the AllSeer had come to see.

He stepped outside, and his foot ground the ash beneath him to fine dust. A door beneath the ash opened, and the AllSeer descended into the planet. He needed no lights to see, and none lit the stairs as he moved down them.

He knew the hallways well since he'd been the one to design them. In this way, the AllSeer was a lot like his father. Aurelius had created his halls and his experiments all those years ago. Aurelius operated on his son and daughter, the children from his loins. The AllSeer didn't have children in that fashion, but he had created...*things*.

It had taken much longer than his father's creations, as had the experiments that still weren't done. The AllSeer thought in terms of centuries, not days, not hours. He never knew if the creatures he was now going to see would bear the fruit of murder.

Yet, after what happened to Ajax, he might need to set them loose.

"Let me see them," he told the first researcher who approached him.

"Certainly," the researcher responded. These scientists were slaves. They were not Superior like the AllSeer, but they were held in higher regard than the slaves who worked in residences. These scientists had been bred for certain jobs under the AllSeer's careful eye.

The man led the AllSeer deeper within the rock, where massive cooling systems had been installed to ensure the molten core wouldn't overheat the subjects.

Finally, the AllSeer reached what he had traveled so far to see, a project he'd begun long ago, and one that now looked like it might be a necessity. "Are they ready?"

The first scientist had left after entering this final room. The AllSeer now stood next to another slave. This one was bald with very pale skin as if he'd never emerged from beneath the ground. Maybe he hadn't. He spoke in a high-pitched voice, and he refused to make eye contact with the AllSeer. Rather, he stared longingly at the creatures inside the tank before them.

"Theeeey have been reeeaadyy, master." The slave stretched out his words as he spoke.

The AllSeer stepped closer to the tank. "Will they obey me?"

"Yesssss," the slave responded, remaining two steps behind the AllSeer.

There were three creatures in front of him, and they were unlike anything the universe had ever seen. They were new in their entirety, and the AllSeer wasn't confident about letting them out. Yet, he wasn't sure what choice he had.

"What woooould you have meeeee doooo, Master?" the slave asked.

One of the creatures lunged at another inside the tank, ripping off a limb. A shriek exploded, one that hurt the AllSeer's mind instead of his ears.

The limb rapidly grew back, and the AllSeer thought the creature who'd attacked was chuckling. "Is it laughing?"

"Yessss, Master. They are plaaaaaying."

The third creature floated in the back. All of them had more tentacles than torso.

The creature who'd regrown a limb lashed out at the first attacker. The second creature tried to move but wasn't fast enough. It was sliced in half, yet it continued to give that odd chuckle. Within a few moments, the second half had rejoined the first, and everything was back to normal in the tank, except for the black blood floating on the water.

The AllSeer placed his hand on the tank. The three creatures on the other side ripped through the water, the oil-colored eyes along all their tentacles focusing on the new hand. Each of the three placed the end of one of their tentacles on the other side of the glass.

"They know you, Maaaasster," the slave said. "You are in theeeeeem, as you are in all of usssss."

The AllSeer took his hand off the tank and turned to look at the slave, a massive being standing over a pathetically small one. "They're ready, then?"

The slave nodded without looking at him, staring at the creatures as if they were his children.

"Release them."

"What shall I use for them to track?"

The AllSeer reached into a pocket on his vest. He pulled out a small vial containing a red liquid and handed it to the slave. "Give them this."

The slave gently took the vial and brought it up to his face. He didn't dare ask what it was. To question the AllSeer would surely mean death. After looking at it for the briefest of moments, he pocketed it. "May I be excused, Master?"

"Give it to them," the AllSeer responded.

The slave rushed out of the AllSeer's view. A few minutes passed, then the AllSeer watched as those tiny red droplets from the vial were pumped into the back of the tank. The creatures' tentacles paused as if sensing something was different. A half-second passed, then the three creatures swarmed. The red liquid disappeared in a flurry of movement as the beings consumed it.

A hole opened on the left side of the tank. The AllSeer watched as the creatures rushed to it, intent on finding the one who'd created the red liquid.

Which was, of course, the Prophesied One.

CHAPTER NINE

Alistair stood on the bridge with Faitrin at his side. The screens in front of them showed the planet that they'd soon land on. The final month of the trip had been relatively painless, a time Alistair had enjoyed and told his council to enjoy as well. The gigantes did as they were told, none venturing to offer an opinion besides Caesar.

The giant had been quiet for a week or so after Alistair spoke with him.

He'd come around at some point and asked a very simple question. "I would like to call you boss instead of master. Is that okay with you?"

Alistair smiled and said "boss" was fine by him. A person could quit a boss.

The dreadnought was outside the planet's gravitational pull, and when questioned by the planet's authorities, it had given coordinates to another part of the galaxy as their destination. The authorities ignored them after that, even though the dreadnought had slowed down considerably.

"You're quiet, Faitrin," Alistair said as they stared at the screens. "You want to tell me what you're thinking?"

The pilot's eyes weren't gray for once. The Terram had loaned Alistair other pilots who were harmonized with the ship at the moment. Men and women alike, they were shorter and stronger than the average human. All seemed more than happy to be on board. The fealty they'd pledged had quickly filtered down through all levels of society. Alistair still didn't understand their language, but it turned out most Terram understood his. They'd just been making it hard on him by not speaking it.

Faitrin was quiet for a few minutes, and Alistair didn't push it. He knew the pilot was worried and not about the possibility of death. This was something else, something more serious bothering her.

"I'm worried about Thoreaux."

Alistair towered over the woman by almost three feet, but when she spoke, it was as if they were equals. The weight of her words hung around his neck like an anvil. "Because of what happened?"

"Yes, because of what *happened*." Her words were venomous. "He's not well, Pro, and if he knew I was talking to you like this... I don't even want to think of the consequences. So you make sure this stays between us."

"Of course," he whispered. The Terram pilots were too far away to hear the discussion, and no one besides him had access to the cameras on the ship. "What's wrong?"

Thoreaux had been distant, much more so than before he was kidnapped. The plan with the planet of gigantes was for Alistair, Thoreaux, and Caesar to make their way down in a smaller pod and figure out the lay of the land.

Obs would stay aboard the dreadnought. Caesar said the terrain was simply not suitable for the drathe. If they could free the gigantes by themselves, then they would. If not, Alistair would bank on himself to come up with a plan.

The usual.

"He's harsher, Pro. Whatever that bitch did to him, he isn't willing or able to let it go. You taking him down there frightens me. It should frighten you, too."

"I can't believe Thoreaux would ever do something to harm me or Caesar," Alistair responded.

Faitrin laughed without looking at him. "I'm not talking about *you*. I'm scared of what he'll do to his enemies, Pro. I love the man. I've loved him almost since the first moment I saw him, just like I knew I'd follow you until I die. You know how I kept saying you'd have to give me whatever I want? All I wanted was him, and now I have him. Even if it's a different version than the one I first met. I don't care. He's dangerous now, Pro. To anyone that stands in your way, he's dangerous."

Alistair remained quiet for a few minutes, thinking about what she said. He thought the truth of her fear lay in what she didn't say. How was he dangerous?

"Thanks, Faitrin," he told her. "I'm going to prepare for our takeoff. I'll keep in mind what you told me."

The pilot said nothing as Alistair walked off. Her words were much simpler than the tumult he felt.

THE WRITTEN HISTORY OF THE GREAT INSURRECTION

Fear.

I know that those who served with me after Helanus vi Thraxus felt it. I know Faitrin felt it. I was different. I had changed.

As we prepared for on the gigante's home planet, I was thinking about it too.

The cruelty on the planet beneath us had only existed in the worst parts of humanity. Slavery. It dated back to our beginnings, and no matter how we tried to rid ourselves of it, we didn't seem to be able to.

The gigantes weren't human, but they were slaves, and somehow the corporation that owned them thought because they'd created the new species, it was okay to enslave them.

The people I fought with were scared because they didn't understand me anymore.

I couldn't tell them at the time, but their fear was actually because they did understand me.

They'd seen what I'd gone through.

DAVID BEERS & MICHAEL ANDERLE

The SkinSuit was a primitive technology that Alistair and his company used out of necessity. The Terram had lent him tech at a very basic level before, but after seeing Alistair's capabilities and his willingness to kill with them, they'd pledged their fealty. That had led to better tech, better than a group of refugees running across the universe could come up with by themselves.

Thoreaux was trying on the new armor when Prometheus came to his room.

The SkinSuit folded up as one item, able to retract from the arms, legs, or torso. The Terram called their battle suit a Fire Starter. The name related to their planet, and the technology was a marvel in its own right.

The armor came in pieces: legs, arms, hands, torso, and finally a helmet. However, the plates melded into one another. Each piece was a part of the whole and formed a single unit.

Thoreaux stood inside the armor with everything but the helmet on. It sat on his bed as he looked at this new tech, wondering how much damage it could deal.

The SkinSuit adapted to cold and heat, allowing people to survive in space and still move with agility.

This was the armor of old, of Roman legions, of American armies before the Ascendancy took over.

Thoreaux didn't understand the tech, but his body was covered with some sort of metal alloy that felt light and supple enough to allow normal movement. He knelt, the knee joints feeling natural. He placed his hand on the deck. This was the test. He'd seen MechSuits in action, but they were huge and clunky. They sped up a wearer's actions and increased their strength, but they lacked the nuances this Fire Starter armor was supposed to possess.

Gripping the floor, he squeezed. He felt no extra pressure inside the suit, and he watched with amazement as the deck bent beneath the force.

Thoreaux pulled his hand back and stared in amazement at the five dimples in the deck. The suit had turned him superhuman.

A knock on the door caused him to turn his head. A small screen on the side showed him Prometheus was standing outside. "Open the door, Jeeves."

The AI was silent, but the door slid open. Thoreaux stood as Pro entered. He was wearing his Fire Starter armor and carrying his helmet.

"Testing it out?" Pro asked.

Thoreaux looked down at the slightly bent deck. "Yeah. It's really something. How does it compare to MechSuits?"

"We haven't used it in battle yet, so I can't say for sure. I know it beats the hell out of SkinSuits, though. I just checked on Caesar. He's almost ready, so I wanted to spin by and see if you are."

Thoreaux hadn't looked up yet, but he knew Pro hadn't shown up here to see if he was ready. They had a drop time, and it wasn't like Thoreaux would miss it. "She said something, didn't she?"

Pro didn't answer the question, and Thoreaux knew what that meant. Faitrin *had* said something. He wasn't angry since he understood her concerns.

"I'm just wondering where your head's at," Prometheus responded.

"Right here on my shoulders." Thoreaux looked up from the deck. "I'm in the game. You don't need to worry about me."

Prometheus stared at him in silence for a few seconds. Finally, he asked, "You'll tell me if you need anything from me, right?"

Thoreaux nodded. "I'm good. If I weren't, I'd tell you."

Pro took one last measure of him, then nodded. "See you at drop time."

The two left it at that, and Pro walked out of the room. Thoreaux finished packing the few items he was bringing onto the foreign world. He knew she'd show up, so he waited.

His back was to the door when she entered. She was quiet, and he didn't turn around.

"He told you I said something, huh?" Faitrin finally asked. She was able to tell the difference in him just from his stance.

"No, he didn't, but he didn't have to." He turned and met her eyes. "What did you tell him?"

"That I was worried about you."

"What are you worried about?"

Faitrin sighed and stepped farther into the room. She walked around Thoreaux and sat on the bed. Leaning forward, she placed her elbows on her knees. "I'm worried about what you're going to do to your enemies."

That wasn't what he'd expected. "What do you mean?"

"I'm worried that you might become like them and not the man I love. I'm worried that what they did to you might have changed you irrevocably."

Thoreaux wasn't sure what to say. She was right. He'd

been changed when his skin was peeled down to the bone. When he was made to cry and beg and sell out his friends. "I don't know what you want from me, Fai."

There were tears in her eyes. "I want you to keep your soul through all of this. I want you to be the kind man I first met. You were a warrior, but it wasn't blood you wanted. It was righteousness."

Thoreaux looked down at the deck. He was silent for what felt like a long time, and Faitrin said nothing. "I'm sorry, Fai. I love you, but I can't undo the past. I can't change what was done to me."

"I don't want you to change what was done to you," she responded. "I want you to change how you react to it."

Thoreaux grabbed his bag and helmet. He stepped to the bed and kissed her cheek lightly. "I love you. I'll be back soon."

CHAPTER TEN

The drop was one of the most uncomfortable ones Alistair had ever experienced. It was easily the fastest, combined with the hardest landing, all of it to ensure the corporation that owned this planet wouldn't see them as anything but a natural phenomenon, if they saw anything.

The ship was the smallest Alistair had ever been in. It was a simple tube the three of them fitted into head to toe. It was aerodynamic, with both ends forming points, and it contained a stealth device that blocked casual viewers from seeing it. The ship was made to launch only once, so structural integrity was not a priority.

Alistair vomited into the tube as they landed, his stomach unable to handle the jolting any longer. The vomit hit the glass in front of his face, then dripped back down onto him, coating his new armor with the contents of his stomach.

The ship stopped moving, and Alistair was on his back. "Son of a bitch," he muttered as saliva hit his forehead.

"Yeah," Thoreaux said over the comm. "That was less than fun."

"Caesar, you good?" Alistair asked.

"I'm fine," the giant responded.

Above Alistair, the doors opened. Alistair's faceplate closed quickly, sensing a slightly different atmosphere than the one inside the bullet ship, which also meant Alistair couldn't wipe away the vomit on his face until the suit identified if the new atmosphere was safe.

He pulled himself out of the bullet ship and stood. A heads-up display inside the helmet said it was nearly done with the atmosphere test. Thoreaux and Caesar both rose from the ship too and stood next to him.

"So, Caesar, exactly where in Hades are we?" Thoreaux asked.

The same question was on Alistair's mind. They were supposed to land on the lightly forested outskirts of a city, but this was something entirely different. They were in a jungle.

Alistair looked above him and saw the tops of tall trees burning where the ship had fallen through. Unseen animals were screeching, either in pain or alerting others to the intrusion. Alistair scanned the area in front of him and saw nothing but plant life stretching as far as the eye could see. The colors were unlike anything he'd seen before, the deepest hues of purple, blue, red, and orange. There was very little green or the brown of tree trunks.

"This is not good," Caesar responded.

"Why is that?"

Caesar knelt and placed his hand on what appeared to

be dirt, although it was a shockingly bright yellow. "We're in the middle of the Institute."

The HUD registered that the atmosphere was acceptable, and Alistair immediately opened the faceplate. He stuck his hand inside, the finger armor peeling back on itself to let him wipe away the vomit. He did the best he could, tossing it violently to the ground while Thoreaux did the same. "You want to clarify that a bit, Caesar?" Alistair asked. "We're supposed to be near the capital, not in a jungle."

"All I know is that we're in the battlegrounds. Most likely, scouts have already seen us and are heading this way. They probably think this is some kind of game the makers are playing. They will not let us simply crash-land into the institute."

Alistair didn't understand how that was possible. He activated the comm to the dreadnought. "Servia, Faitrin, Relm, this is Prometheus. Do you have our location?"

Everyone waited for an answer, but after a minute, none had come.

"Jeeves," Alistair asked. "Jeeves, are you hearing me?"

Again, no answer came. They were cut off from the ship and their AI. Caesar was still kneeling, feeling the earth. Alistair turned to him. "What happens when the scouts find us, Caesar?"

"They'll either kill us here or incapacitate us and drag us back to their domain. From there, they will probably torture us until we tell them what they want to hear, which will most likely be that the other clans inside the Institute sent us."

"Well, that sounds great," Thoreaux said. He was slowly

scanning the perimeter, letting his HUD tell him what it could see. "Personally, I've had enough torture for my lifetime, so I'm going to pass on it. Pro, what's the plan?"

Alistair could only come up with one answer to what had happened. The corporation had seen through their maneuver, and rather than blast them out of the sky, they had altered their landing plans and sent them into the middle of this school's game. That, or somehow Jeeves had managed to fuck up the entire landing, which didn't seem possible.

"For right now, we've got to get away from this bullet ship. Caesar, what exactly are you doing on the ground?"

"Understanding where the gigantes are. They seem to have fled but are pausing."

Alistair didn't understand how that was possible, but he knew the giant wasn't lying to him. "Do you know where we can hide for a bit?"

"Maybe." The giant stood. "I haven't been here for years, but it's possible the place is still there. Come. Follow me."

The giant was the only one not wearing Fire Starter armor. The Terram didn't have anything near his size, plus the giant felt more comfortable in his own armor.

Alistair and Thoreaux followed him as he moved through the dense jungle. The giant was extremely agile, able to move around the vines and plants like he was an Earth-born monkey and not a creature even bigger than Alistair.

They walked silently for a long time, or as silently as they could. The unseen animals above let out screeches from time to time, alerting the other creatures to these newcomers.

"How far away are we?" Alistair asked. His HUD showed they'd walked over six miles already and that three hours had passed.

"Almost there," the giant said.

"What happens if the place isn't as you remember it?" Thoreaux asked.

"We will most likely die," Caesar responded, sounding as frightened as he always did in these circumstances. Which was to say, not at all.

"I should start asking this stuff before we begin the journey," Thoreaux remarked.

They walked another half-mile and then the jungle opened before them. They stood on the face of a cliff, staring off at a river that Alistair's HUD said was over a mile wide. The drop was nearly a third of a mile, and to Alistair, it looked as if something was swimming upstream in the waters.

"Where do we go from here?" Alistair asked.

"Down," the giant said. He squatted on the edge of the cliff, then flipped over the edge. Alistair jumped forward, about to scream, then saw the giant quickly climbing down. His hands and feet caught the rocks necessary to descend almost without him looking.

Thoreaux stepped up next to Alistair and watched the giant moving down. "I'm glad you didn't have to fight him on this cliff face. I don't think he would have joined us."

"Thanks for your vote of confidence," Alistair said. "I can tell you one thing I don't like about this armor already. It doesn't have jetpacks on the boots."

They were going to have to climb, just like the gigante.

Very slowly and carefully, Alistair lowered himself

down the cliff face. Caesar was already a quarter of the way down, not looking at them. Thoreaux came behind Alistair, slightly to the left to prevent rocks from falling on his head.

Ten minutes into their glacially paced descent, Alistair checked to see where Caesar was. He couldn't see him anywhere, and the giant didn't appear to have dropped to his death below. "*CAESAR!*" Alistair shouted.

There was no response for twenty seconds or so. Alistair didn't move but scanned the area below. He glanced up and saw Thoreaux doing the same.

The shot nearly took off his right shoulder. Rock exploded next to him, then stones were falling on his head. Alistair looked up quickly and saw Thoreaux hanging by one arm from a jutting boulder.

"Go!" he shouted. "I'm fine."

Another shot pulverized the rock below him, and Alistair started moving. Hand over hand, foot over foot, he rushed down the rock. Something tagged his right calf, and the HUD said it weakened the armor there by fifty percent. Alistair ignored it all, including the shots coming every few seconds. He figured the only way they were missing was that they were on the other side of the river, miles away.

He had no idea where he was going, rushing down in a mad sprint, hoping to find safety somewhere below.

The yell above him told him what was happening before he saw it. Alistair's head jerked up as Thoreaux fell past him, a shot having made him lose purchase on the cliff face. Alistair didn't think, he simply reacted. He leaned off the cliff, letting go with his left arm, and grabbed Thoreaux's outstretched forearm as he passed.

The weight was too much even for Alistair's superior strength, and physics pulled him off. He didn't release Thoreaux as he felt his right hand lose its grip and his feet start to slip.

Then they were both falling, the HUD reading distance and moments to impact. Alistair's body remained calm as it always did, his mind telling him their armor would be crushed on impact, along with the two of them.

Then, as if from nowhere, two massive hands reached out and grabbed them. Alistair felt as if a god had grabbed him as he was wrenched sideways, surely to be broken against the cliff face.

Instead, he was flung backward and hit the ground, skidding across it. He reacted as quickly as he could, pulling his Whip free as he rolled to a crouching position, the red tentacles circling in the air.

The enemy before him was smiling. Caesar. "In this jungle, never yell no matter what. Death is always listening."

The three of them were in a cavern that was hidden in the cliff. Because of the distance from the cliff to land, it looked like another piece of rock with no hole to climb inside.

Caesar had found it when he was young while he was being chased through the jungle above. His pursuers thought he'd fallen off and been washed away by the river, but he'd hidden there.

Alistair had been right; the shots were coming from the

other side of the river. Scouts must have been placed there, and the shout had made them scan the cliff.

"Are they going to try to find us?" Alistair asked once he was sure no one was injured, including Caesar. Regardless of how great a warrior Alistair was, he would never come close to the giant's strength.

"Most definitely," Caesar responded.

"This is bad," Thoreaux said. "Like, really bad. We have no contact with the dreadnought, no contact with Jeeves, and only the gods know how many giants are chasing us."

Caesar was standing at the edge of the cavern, staring beyond the river. "One thousand."

"Huh?" Thoreaux asked.

"One thousand gigantes are coming after us. Each year, one thousand are bred. This planet is large enough for five classes to attend the Institute at once. We are in groupings of five hundred versus five hundred. By now, word is spreading to the Magnus on both sides."

"I'm going to assume," Alistair said, "that Magnus is the person in command."

"You assume correctly." The gigante didn't sound worried. If anything, he sounded contemplative.

Alistair stepped up next to him. "I need your help, Caesar. What do we do from here?"

"I'm considering," the giant remarked without looking at him. "If we wait here, they will find us. I am sure of that. I nearly died here, and it was only through this place I was able to rise to Magnus."

Thoreaux came up on Alistair's right side. "You were the greatest of your group?"

Caesar looked at him. "I was Magnus of my clan, and

Lord Magnus over the entire Institute. There was none higher than me at my graduation."

Thoreaux's faceplate was retracted, and Alistair saw him smile. "Sorry, sorry, big man. I didn't mean to ruffle any feathers. I believe ya."

Caesar stared at him for another second as if not trusting the mea culpa. Finally, he looked back over the river. "Strength can be built from secrecy. That was what I did after I nearly died in here. If we want to survive, we must build strength. It is all the gigantes will follow. There are five thousand gigantes on this planet fighting wars right now. Many will die, most likely half in each part of the institute. Without air support from the council, we will have to win over this institute first."

"What do you mean?" Thoreaux asked.

Alistair understood. "He means we're going to have to kill gigantes until they decide to follow us. I got that about right, Caesar?"

The giant was solemn as he answered. "Unfortunately, for now, that is the only way. Some must die so the rest can be free."

Alistair looked at Caesar. He saw sadness on the giant's face, an emotion he wasn't sure he'd seen from the giant. He understood it, though, or he thought he did.

Since Caesar finally understood freedom, he could finally feel sympathy for those bred like him. He realized what he needed to do, and he hated that he would have to do it.

CHAPTER ELEVEN

The cave they'd entered wound back into the cliff and down a slope that twisted back around to the river. It took the three of them an hour to walk down to it, and when Alistair had tried to unholster his Whip, Caesar told him not to.

"Light, noise, both are dangerous on this world. It is best to move silently in darkness."

They found themselves about six miles up from the river, and Alistair marveled at the color. The purple rush ran below him, and now that he was closer, he could see the creatures swimming upstream. They weren't fish like one would see on Earth. They appeared to be giant eels. Each one stretched at least three feet long, and they kept a wide distance from each other.

"What are they?" Alistair asked.

"They're what's protecting us right now," Caesar answered. "This river divides the two clans. Those down there are waiting for someone to try and cross. Someone who thinks they're brave and wants to show how strong they are."

Caesar's eyes widened. He raised a hand and pointed about fifty yards on the right.

"There. He will try to come over here and find us. He thinks it's his way to glory. Once he enters the river, we will cross."

"We're going to cross the river?" Thoreaux asked. "The one with those big eel things that are supposedly keeping us safe?"

"We can't go back up," Caesar answered. "The other clan is most likely at the top of the cliff and moving down. They will find the lair soon, then they will find us here. The only path to survival is forward across the river. Swim strong and fast. The brave up there will do the rest for us."

Alistair took a step closer to the edge. The giant was almost at the river, and it was as if the eel-like creatures could smell him. Alistair could see they were surging forward through the purple water, moving closer to each other as at least ten of them tried to get upstream fast enough. The giant was a young brave, showing none of the scars that littered Caesar's body. Looking at the eels, Alistair didn't see any way that the brave would make it, nor would he be able to heal himself with the nanotechnology in his hands.

It was a fool's errand that would only end in death, all to prove he was the strongest.

"Wait for my command," Caesar said. "Then we go. Do not look upstream or down. Only at the other side."

"Have you ever done this?" Thoreaux asked.

Caesar nodded. "Once." That was all he said, and there wasn't time to ask more questions.

Alistair's faceplate was closed, and he was watching the massive brave standing on the river's edge. He wore armor different from Caesar's. It was newer and left his arms and head exposed. The brave was quiet, not boasting or screaming, and that made Alistair feel more pity for him. On this world, the only way to greatness was foolish tasks like this. To show yourself the strongest so evil men could buy and sell you later for greater sums of currency.

They were coming to kill Alistair now, and he was going to kill as many of them as it took to free them.

The brave held a laser blade in each hand. He didn't appear to be trying to out-swim the beasts coming for him but to cut them down.

He stepped into the water.

"*Go*," Caesar whispered harshly. He jumped off the ledge, and Thoreaux followed, both hitting the ground. Alistair didn't move. He watched the brave.

The young gigante sliced through the water with his blades. Steam rose from the lasers and the sound of screeching tires filled the air. It could only be the screams of the dying eels. The purple water ahead was suddenly stained with red. The brave began marching forward, his eyes on the water.

Alistair remained where he was as his friends touched the river.

Thoreaux turned back to look at him, and Alistair knew waiting like this was endangering everyone. He still couldn't pull away.

The first eel to make contact launched out of the water

like a missile shot. It came from behind the brave and caught his left shoulder. The creature's mouth opened wide, and Alistair saw long, needle-like teeth that couldn't possibly fit in their owner's mouth. The eyes were cold and dead as if seeing nothing and everything at the same time.

The eel grabbed the brave's shoulder, its teeth sinking through flesh, tendon, and bone. The brave let out a horrific scream as his arm was separated from his body and hit the water.

Alistair moved then.

He catapulted off the ledge, hit the ground in a somersault, and was back on his feet, rushing for the water. Caesar had not entered yet. He stood at the edge, shaking his head at Alistair's stupidity.

The three hit the purple river at the same time.

The water rushed over Alistair, pushing him downstream of the massacre. He swam as fast as he could, the suit helping to propel him. The helmet processed the water and allowed oxygen in.

Alistair tried looking upstream, but the transparent purple water had turned opaque red, all of it flooding toward him. The brave's blood had mixed with that of the eels he'd killed.

The screams had stopped, and that meant only one thing. The eels were feasting but would soon come for them.

Alistair swam faster, unable to tell where his friends were. He looked upstream every few strokes and let his HUD tell him of any dangers. He was a quarter-mile from the riverbank when it spotted the first eel.

Incoming, twenty seconds.

Alistair didn't try to swim faster. He knew it would be futile. Rather, he stood against the rushing river, fully realizing that brave's strength for the first time. Even with his armor on, the rushing water nearly toppled him. The eel launched from the water just as its brother had earlier. Alistair's Whip was faster than the brave's blade, and the lasers sliced the thing's head off. It gave that awful scream.

Incoming, five seconds, his HUD read.

Alistair didn't have any idea where it was coming from. Certainly not upstream.

He turned, facing downstream and hoping his armor had sensed it. The creature's head was at his, the needle teeth inches from his helmet. Alistair ducked, and the river bowled him over. He hit the eel's middle, and the creature wrapped itself around him like an anaconda. They tumbled downriver, Alistair barely holding onto his Whip with his right hand while he fended off the snapping creature with his left.

The thing's dead eyes belied its intelligence and instinct. It wrapped itself around Alistair's midsection, trying to lever his ribs into his internal organs while its teeth snapped at his helmet. Alistair couldn't get a purchase on the riverbed. He tumbled over and over, his head going beneath the water before coming up briefly. He felt his way against the eel, using all his strength to keep the fully-muscled body from decapitating him. Despite his helmet delivering oxygen, his lungs couldn't suck any in. The armor was keeping the creature from breaking his ribs, but he couldn't expand his lungs.

He had to kill it. That was the only way to make it out of this.

If there was any way to. More had to be swimming at him at this very second.

Alistair let go of the eel's head with his left arm, letting the creature lunge for his helmet. It was the only way to get his right hand close enough and was a gamble that would end in death for one of them.

The eel's teeth hit his helmet on the right side as his Whip sliced through its flesh.

He felt the lower half go limp, the screech filling his ears. The head was still on his helmet, the needles having pierced the metal, but Alistair ripped the lower portion off while tumbling downriver.

He hit the riverbed, the eel's head dislodging from his helmet.

Incoming, five seconds.

Alistair felt the strength drain from his body. He swung the Whip forward blindly, slicing through red water and having no idea if he was hitting anything. Something grabbed his left arm at the same time something wrapped around his left leg.

Then he was wrenched free of the river. A giant's hand was on his left bicep. Alistair had no idea if belonged to friend or foe, but he knew what the gray tube around his leg was.

The eel's head rushed for Alistair's throat, and he cut it in two with his Whip. The head kept flying forward, screaming, and hit his shoulder before falling to the ground, its jaw weakly opening and closing.

Alistair hit the ground right after it *hard*. He instinctively brought his Whip up, ready to cut down whatever was on him, and only in the last second pulled it back. It was Caesar.

"Stupid, boss. Stupid, stupid, boss. You nearly *died*."

Alistair let his body relax, falling limply against the yellow soil. His Whip retracted, and he stared at the green sky. Blue clouds floated across it.

"Stupid," the giant said again before standing.

"He's right," Thoreaux responded, walking toward the two of them. "What the hell were you thinking, Pro?"

He watched the clouds, unmoving. "I thought someone should watch him die. It was a brave act."

"Well," Caesar said, "yours was a stupid act. Come. Get up. We have to move quickly."

Alistair knew the giant was right. He slowly got to his feet. "Run a damage check," he told his armor. An outline of his suit appeared on the HUD. He'd taken damage on both calves and his torso, but surprisingly not his helmet. The eel had barely sunk his teeth into it.

"Thoreaux, aren't you supposed to be watching my six, my blind areas?"

"Blind areas aren't stupid areas, Pro," his second said from ahead of him.

True enough, Alistair thought and followed his friends into the jungle.

Twelve men and women sat around a long, rectangular table. Each had a DataTrack in front of them and was staring at the New Ganges River. Each felt they had just witnessed something impossible, and for the first time, each felt a twinge of fear.

The man at the head of the table's name was Binsum Tinsert Immorium Dax. Everyone in his life referred to him as Bin, or Lord Dax, depending on the relationship.

Binsum Tinsert Immorium Dax was staring at something he'd never thought would happen. The entire scene he had just witnessed struck him as, well, something out of a dream.

To sum it up, a dreadnought had shot a missile-like vessel at their planet. It had been shot too quickly for the planet's defensive systems to react beyond sending sonic waves to alter its original landing spot. They had managed to place it inside one of the Institute's war ranges, and Bin had hoped that would be enough.

However, more of this dream came next. One of the gigantes who had been crowned Lord Magnus stepped out of the ship, along with two strange men Bin had never seen before.

They proceeded to fall down a cliff, avoid rifle fire, and then... Well, perhaps out of everything, that was the most improbable part. The New Ganges River had been built, and the eels in it bred so the overly brave and dumb gigantes would try to cross it to prove their worth. The eels were bloodthirsty monsters that had ripped apart everyone who'd tried crossing except the *returned* gigante. However, even he hadn't killed an eel, but this new man had killed several before being ripped out of the water.

Now they had crossed the river, the dead bodies of gigante and eels alike floating downstream, and the satellites had lost sight of them in the jungle.

More, this man who had killed multiple eels—which should be impossible by Bin's standards—held a weapon Bin had only heard about in stories. The legendary Whip, carried by Titans on Earth.

"I'm a bit confused," Thera said from the head of the table. "Can anyone explain to me what we just witnessed? Perhaps you can, Alrain?"

Alrain was an older gentleman who had been with the company since Bin's father founded it. He was head of security and had assured everyone at this table that the Ganges would stop the group. The old man was now slumped in his chair, looking at the forest in front of him— one he *could* see into. Slowly, he straightened. "I believe you saw what I just did, Thera. So you can keep your judgments to yourself. Nothing like that has ever happened in the history of this company."

"I—" Thera started.

"Stop, both of you," Bin said. "Bickering right now isn't going to change anything we just witnessed." Bin's father had stepped down years ago, and in a way Bin didn't necessarily trust. It was unexpected and left him with a company board full of people he hadn't chosen, who were probably still loyal to his father. The infighting was worse than Bin had imagined, but until now, he'd needed these old people to help him navigate a company he'd thought he'd have another twenty years to learn about. "Do we know who the other two are yet? They've had the faceplates off multiple times. What are the facial scanners saying?"

Verish, sitting next to Bin, tapped the DataTrack, and two faces showed up in front of Bin's. "The man on the left is named Alistair Kane. What you saw him fighting with wasn't a fake. He's a former Titan, and from what InterGal says, he is wanted by the Commonwealth. The man on the right is a run-of-the-mill Subversive, also wanted by the Commonwealth, but he's only known due to his length of time with the Subversives. This Kane is a high-value target."

"Great. The Commonwealth has no dominion out here," Bin said. "So can someone please fucking tell me what the hell they're doing here with a gigante?"

No one at the table said anything. Everyone stared at the two faces in front of them, either reading—or pretending to read—the brief bios presented.

"All this high-paid fucking talent sitting here, and no one can tell me anything?" Bin spat.

Again, the table remained silent. Bin rubbed his hand roughly across his face. "Alrain," he said as he placed his hand back on the table. "What are the chances of them surviving the clan?"

The old man glanced over from the other end of the table. "I would have said zero, but I just told you the chance of them crossing the Ganges was zero, and clearly I was wrong there."

This was giving Bin a godsdamn headache. He had a business to run. "And the dreadnought above? Any word from them?"

"Silence," Thera responded. "They clearly understand we've cut off all communications between them and their three entrants, but they aren't responding to us, nor are they moving closer to the planet."

Bin leaned back in his chair. "Well, I'm certainly not meeting with the bastards. Whatever they want here, it isn't business that pays in credit. Send an envoy down there and have it talk to the Titan. This is all completely out of control. We've got five Institutes running, and I don't have time to deal with this insanity." Bin looked around the table. "Any questions?"

Everyone at the table shook their head. This might be the first opportunity for him to fire some of these ancients. All the infighting and bickering might end with these newcomers, and regardless of what they wanted, Bin wasn't going to let them get off the fucking planet.

Alistair kept his somewhat damaged armor on because the heat on the planet was awful. The suit kept him cool, but Caesar looked miserable.

They trampled through the jungle. Alistair didn't ask where they were going. He'd learned his lesson about moving silently. Caesar would tell him what he needed to know when the time was right. Beyond anything else, they didn't want to get ambushed in this jungle.

He kept his Whip at the ready, sometimes cutting down vines and plants that blocked their way.

Alistair's HUD kept up with the time they'd spent moving. About two hours into their hike, Caesar paused.

"What is it?" Thoreaux whispered, in the middle between Alistair and the giant.

Caesar turned his head toward the sky. Alistair followed his look, and the armor allowed him to hear what Caesar already did. Some sort of copter was flying overhead.

"The makers," Caesar whispered. His face was full of awe, and he got down on his knees as the sound of the copter grew louder.

Alistair stepped next to his friend and placed a hand on his shoulder. "There's no need to bow. Not to them, the makers, or anyone else. Stand up with me. Be on your feet when they arrive."

Caesar was still staring at the sky. He blinked a few times as if Alistair's words were sinking into him, then found his leader's eyes. "They are the makers. They kill indiscriminately. They will kill us for coming here."

"They're not going to kill me, Caesar. Not here in this overgrown jungle. Please, do not meet them on your knees. Meet them on your feet like a free gigante."

Caesar dropped his eyes, and it was obvious how much of a struggle it was for him to get to his feet. A mental thing, not physical, because of how badly these men had treated him and how badly they still treated the creatures living on this planet. Slowly, Caesar returned to his feet, though he didn't look fierce about it.

The sound of the copter grew louder, and Alistair finally saw it above the canopy. It hung in the air for a few seconds. He watched as five humanoid beings jumped out of the side with ropes attached to them. They crashed through the canopy, breaking branches and vines alike without a care for the damage they caused.

We're not dealing with humans, Alistair thought, knowing that bones and armor would have been broken or damaged in such a fast fall.

They landed about fifty feet in front of Alistair's group, and he saw the ropes that connected them to the copter were metal strands. The beings in front of him were droids, though not like any Alistair had ever seen.

Thoreaux either. "What am I looking at here, big man?"

"The maker's servants," Caesar whispered, unable to shake the mysteries from his childhood. The *myths*.

The droids had pointed heads that formed a beak instead of a mouth. Their eyes were bright green, and their metal exoskeletons blended with the environment around them, turning the exotic colors of this strange jungle. It would make them great killing machines if they had to go up against the giants.

Alistair stepped forward, his Whip at his side. Thoreaux had unholstered the MechPulse from his leg. Alistair wasn't concerned about a battle here. He and Thoreaux could take out these five by themselves if Caesar couldn't get over his past. If they'd wanted to kill him, they would have sent more.

The droid looked at Caesar for a moment, something akin to disdain on his metal face. "You dare not bow to me, servant?"

Caesar said nothing, but he did step forward, joining the other two.

So the droids had cognition or something approaching it. "We bow to nothing," Alistair said. "Why are you here?"

The other droids formed a semi-circle around the one in the middle, their metal skins adapting to the colors of the jungle around them. The middle one spoke. "That is the question my masters want answered. Why are you here? And you, servant? Why have you returned?"

"We're here for the rest of his kind," Alistair told the metal creature.

It paused for a moment and looked at those standing next to it. "That's not computing for any of us," it said after a second. "Can you say it in a different way?"

Now it sounded like a computer, not a petulant child. Alistair's Whip dropped farther toward the ground. "I came here to free the gigantes. All of your Institutes will fall. Your labs where they're bred. Everything is going to crumble before I leave."

The droid was quiet for a second. Its eye lit up bright green when it spoke. "I've recorded the answer, but I haven't transferred it yet. Are you sure that's what you want me to respond with?"

Alistair nodded. "Tell whoever sent you that we're coming for them."

The droid cocked its head to the side. "I have heard of suicidal creatures but never met one. We are well met."

The metal cords pulled the droids back up to the copter, leaving the space before Alistair empty. Alistair looked up, watching as the droids were rushed away at a speed that would have injured most men.

"Maybe a more diplomatic tone would have been better," Thoreaux said from his right.

Alistair turned to look at Caesar. The giant was walking deeper into the jungle. "Come," he instructed from ahead. "This place is marked for death now. We must hurry."

The giant, though he didn't think of himself in that way, saw the maker's servants land. He listened from a safe distance, more than shocked that someone would speak to the servants like that. When he was younger, the giant had seen someone cut down for daring to glance at the servants. Since then, no one the giant knew had ever dared look at them.

Speaking to them in that fashion was...*blasphemous.*

The giant didn't know the other of his kind who led the humans away. He knew the humans were wearing strange armor he'd never seen before, but he didn't concern himself about that.

He'd liked the way the human had spoken to the servants. He realized the entire place would be in flames soon, the humans and the large one with it, but he couldn't help but enjoy it.

Such talk was why he was out here hiding on his own. Of course, he would never have dared speak to a servant like that, but to others of his kind? He sometimes found himself unable to keep words like those from escaping his lips.

"This place is marked for death now," the one like him said.

That was the truth. The giant slowly picked his way farther from the group and then took off, knowing very well what was coming toward them all.

Bin was alone in his office, far away from where the human and his lackeys traveled.

"Have the main envoy deactivated and retooled," he told his assistant, who stood in the doorway.

He'd just watched the discussion between the droid and

former Titan. He was looking at the holovid, barely comprehending what he'd just heard. He leaned back in his chair and wondered if the droid was right in his assessment. Was the former Titan suicidal, as well as the other two traveling with him?

"Contact Alrain," he told the AI.

A moment later, the old man's face replaced the Titan's on the holovid. "Yes, sir?"

"I'm sending you the coordinates where we found the intruders. I want you to light the whole place up," he told his head of security.

The old man paused before responding, looking pensive. "Sir, I don't mean to tell you your business, but that will disrupt the game. We've never done anything like this before. I hardly think it necessary to do so over three intruders."

"The game will be fine," Bin responded. "If anything, it'll create a different parameter. We can probably mark the winners up thirty percent from it. Just light the place up, all right? How long will it take?"

Alrain looked away for a few seconds. "Based on the coordinates, we should be able to get a team there in an hour."

"Try to make it quicker. I want that place on fire, and those three burned alive within it."

"I'll do my best, sir," Alrain replied.

Bin shut down the holovid. He stared at the table, thinking about what the man had said. Did he have any idea what he was saying? He was going to try to shut down an intergalactic corporation, one that had unlimited firepower? Bin had never experienced anything that idiotic, yet the man spoke as if his words would become truth.

Well, shortly he would see the truth. Fire would fall from the sky, and this little episode would be over.

"Contact that dreadnought," he told the AI.

A few moments passed, then the computer said, "You're connected."

"This is Lord Binsum Tinsert Immorium Dax. I own the planet you've sent intruders to. After repeated attempts to contact you, this will be the last time I do so. It is now clear that you have attempted to invade our private property, and one of the cretins you just dropped on our peaceful planet has threatened us. Due to the corporation's peaceful nature, we will not be sending an armada to destroy your ship, although we are well within our rights to do so. However, we will be killing those you sent within the next hour. If there is any attempt by your dreadnought to intervene, we will be forced to take drastic measures against it as well."

He paused for a second, letting his anger subside at the sheer audacity of what they were attempting.

"It is in your best interests to leave our airspace. If this aggression continues, you will force our hand. This has been a silly, stupid, and pointless endeavor on your part."

He shut the holovid down, then slammed his flat hand onto the table.

Bin didn't like any of this. He was a businessman. In all his father's time as head of the company, nothing like this had ever happened. Of course, it would be under his reign that something this idiotic happened.

Still, it could be used for his benefit. Bin planned on

upping the cost of the gigantes playing where the fire fell. If they sold at a premium, he saw no reason other types of intrusions couldn't happen. It could create a premium caste of gigante.

Maybe this was a blessing in disguise. He'd find out within an hour.

Servia listened to the transmission coming from the planet beneath. She saw the thin, annoying face of the company's leader on her holovid and wished she could slit his throat. Unfortunately, he was too far out of her reach.

The rest of Pro's council watched the transmission as well: Relm, Faitrin, and the AllMother. Servia had taken over as leader when they left, the AllMother saying that her time leading anyone was done. Still, Servia found herself looking at the old woman when the message was over.

The AllMother stared at where the man's face had been.

Servia didn't say what she was thinking, that the man had been right in his assessment. This was stupid, not to mention deadly. Servia didn't say it because she'd thought that about many of Pro's decisions, and each time he'd come out stronger than before. Their entire movement had. Servia was coming to understand that things that couldn't be accomplished by mere mortals, Pro could make happen.

Even so, this seemed beyond him. He had himself, Thoreaux, and Caesar.

"Does anyone have any thoughts on this?" she asked those at the table.

Relm raised his eyebrows. "I think it might be a good idea to skedaddle on out of this galaxy at least if we're talking about safety."

Faitrin punched him in the arm. "I don't even wanna hear that shit in jest."

He put his hands up in protest. "Okay, okay. Calm down." Placing his arms on the table, he looked at Servia. "I mean, we're not leaving him. So that leaves us two options. We send down the gigantes, or we let him do what he planned."

"The gods dashed that plan the moment the bullet left our dreadnought," she said. "Faitrin, what do you say?"

The pilot was obviously still controlling her emotions. "I say we let Pro continue. I don't think he'd want us to send the gigantes down there and risk their deaths. He seems to have different plans for them."

Servia understood how hard it must have been for her to say that. Right now, she looked like a woman carved from stone, but there wasn't any doubt of the love she felt for Thoreaux.

"AllMother?" Servia turned her attention to their former leader.

The old woman looked up as if she'd been lost in thought and hadn't expected anyone to ask for her opinion. She waved her hand in the air as if to dissipate smoke in front of her. "Whatever you all decide. I'm sleepy, and I think I might lie down for a nap."

Servia raised her eyebrows, not in jest as Relm had, but in surprise. "Mother, you can't be serious."

She yawned and pushed up from her chair. "I am, Servia. I'm very sleepy. Whatever you all decide, I am good with."

Servia watched as the old woman left the room, more than surprised by the move. She was shocked.

The door closed behind the AllMother, leaving the other three on the council alone.

Relm stared at the door. "Does she have dementia or something? I know we pretty much eradicated that as a species, but her age combined with this shit..." He shrugged and looked at Servia. "What do we *do*?"

Servia could unleash the gigantes, and—she'd admit it to herself—that was her first instinct. She had to trust Pro, though. They were out of contact with him, but Faitrin was right. Pro had different designs for the gigantes. If she ruined that, it could destroy his later plans.

If they survived.

"We're going to trust Pro. He'll get out of this."

The AllMother knew the rest of Pro's council thought she was toying with them. She wasn't, though. She was tired and growing more so each day.

She wouldn't claim to understand what Prometheus was doing. She hadn't found him in order to know what he would do. She'd found him to unleash him on the universe, and that was exactly what she had done. Right now, he had been unleashed on an enslavement camp. While their little president might think he had the upper hand, the AllMother knew the truth.

Pro would get out of this. Somehow.

The AllMother was more concerned about herself at this moment. She was coming to wonder something she hadn't thought about before. Would she live to see the revolution?

Would she see her blood lose his iron grip over the human race?

The AllMother made it to her bedroom and laid down.

She closed her eyes and knew that sleep would come soon. Perhaps dreams, too—the dreams of the modified. They had been coming more frequently lately, although she'd said nothing to anyone about it.

The AllMother took a deep breath and let it out slowly. The dreams would come. She didn't want them, but she was tired.

Oh, so tired.

CHAPTER TWELVE

"Alexandria..."

The word rolled across her like ocean waves, each syllable hitting her individually.

Alex, not yet the AllMother in this place, dropped to one knee.

"You know if you die, that won't stop me, right?"

The voice wasn't the changed, morphed, alien voice of the creature who called himself the AllSeer. It was the voice of her brother Alexander before he had become this twisted monster.

"If you die, sister, it will make it easier."

Alex got to her feet. She had been able to explain what was happening to Prometheus because the same thing was happening to her. It was something else she'd kept from those she cared about. So much of her life was a secret that she hardly knew what to tell anyone anymore.

Something flashed in the corner, and Alex's eyes darted to it. Whatever had been there was gone, replaced by shadow.

"I only want you alive so that I can look you in the eye when you finally understand that all of this running, all of these unending years, were for nothing."

Another flash, this one in her peripheral vision. Alex turned quickly, but it was gone.

"I'm going to make him suffer, Alexandria. I'm going to make him hurt worse than you could ever imagine. The things Father inflicted on those he conquered? They will seem like a sweet release compared to what will happen to your Prophesied One."

Alex laughed at that. "Is that so, Alexander? What are you waiting for, then? Your greatest warrior was cut down in mere minutes, even with poison running through my fighter's body. Are you waiting for a better chance? Or do you also want me to see you cut him down? Although that wouldn't make much sense, given I was there to watch the last battle."

The shadow that had been bouncing around in the corners now appeared in front of her. It was massive, like Caesar, and had form and substance. She could see some of her brother's former features, though most of them had changed or were lost in the blackness of this three-dimensional shadow.

It stepped forward far quicker than she could back up. It was upon her, and the shadow opened its mouth. Her brother's perfect teeth were gone, and a black hole confronted her. "I defy time, sister. My Superior Ones are not me. I am what our father wanted to be, what he could not ever become."

Alex wouldn't back up. She wouldn't give an inch to

this bastardization. "Well, brother, you still don't have my warrior or me, so it seems like you're missing something."

The shadow raised a hand as if to backhand her but stopped before it slapped her face.

Alex smiled at the creature. "Why not try it?"

Her brother did nothing, his black jaw flexing with anger.

Alex took a deep breath, and when she breathed out, she did it directly into the shadow's face. Pieces of it broke off, fluttering away and disappearing.

She heard her brother's whisper as he left the shared space.

"I'll see you soon, Alex. Don't die on me. I want you to see me when you meet your fate."

THE WRITTEN HISTORY OF THE GREAT INSURRECTION

This writing will address the AllMother as well as her leadership. Given that I served under her most of my life, I cannot say this is an unbiased account, but something needs to be said about it.

Without the AllMother, there would be no Insurrection. There would be no Prometheus. Alistair Kane would have died a Titan, his name perhaps preserved in some small footnote of history, to eventually be lost in the vastness of space. I, Servia, Faitrin, Relm—no one would have ever known our names beyond those closest to us, and our deaths would have wiped us from humanity's memory.

The gigantes, the Terram, the legions of followers—none of it would exist without her. Looking at human history, I'm not sure anyone ever built anything as vast or strong as she did. I'm not sure such a thing will ever be possible again. What she did was flat-out heroic, and before anything else is said, that is the most important thing.

Looking at what she did from the moment she left

Earth until she was reunited with her brother, her leadership tactics should be evaluated. I imagine military scholars will study her far into the future.

For my part, I will say the AllMother withheld a lot of information from her followers. Truthfully, until Prometheus arrived, she withheld almost everything, only telling those who needed information that would further her ends.

With the vision of hindsight, it's obvious there were things she hid that shouldn't have been kept from us. Things that unduly harmed the insurrection. The greatest was about her brother. She told Prometheus what he wanted, but not everything.

Perhaps he will comment publicly on it one day if we survive.

Or perhaps keeping that from him doomed us all.

We will know soon enough.

CHAPTER THIRTEEN

Five quadcopters whisked overhead. Alistair stopped his dreadful pace through the jungle to stare at the sky through a small break in the canopy. The copters had rushed past but were now slowing down and spreading out to four corners, with one in the middle. The area they were spread over was vast, multiple square miles.

"What's happening?" Alistair yelled to Caesar.

"The makers kill us now," Caesar hollered over his shoulder. He hadn't stopped running. Neither had Thoreaux, although if Caesar was right, it was a futile exercise.

"*STOP!*" Alistair commanded, and he heard his friends come to a halt. He turned to the giant. "Caesar, how are they going to kill us?"

The giant was staring up now as his chest heaved. "Fire."

"Like, right *now?*" Thoreaux asked.

Caesar nodded without looking at either of them. "They're positioning themselves."

"The area is huge," Alistair said. "They're going to burn gigantes too."

Caesar finally tipped his head down. "We are property, same as this land. They can create more."

"Pro," Thoreaux said, "this isn't good."

Alistair had seen something like this before, but that time, they'd had somewhere to escape to. A Portal. Alistair's eyes scanned the jungle around him. There was nothing but yellows, reds, and blues surrounding him. He saw plants of all kinds but *nothing* that would stop the coming fire. He looked across the expanse at Caesar. "Your armor won't protect you, will it? What about the nanotech?"

"They will burn this land until there is nothing left. No armor will protect us. Not yours, not mine."

"Fuck," Alistair whispered into his helmet. He wasn't sure his suit would fail him. Then again, if they just continued to burn, eventually the Fire Starter would falter.

Caesar's head jerked to the right, and he pulled a laser blade from his leg with his left hand and a small gun with his right.

The quadcopter above them moved a little bit to its right, perfecting its location.

"What is it?" Alistair asked, turning in the same direction Caesar had. His HUD scanned the area but wasn't able to see through the dense vegetation.

The first quadcopter unleashed its flames from the far right corner. They shot from a generator on the bottom, streaking through the air and immediately setting the canopy on fire. The flames forced their way down, and unseen animals cried into the air.

"*RUN!*" Alistair shouted, but Caesar didn't move. He held the gun steady on something in the distance even as the second quadcopter unleashed fire onto the world, this one in the top left corner.

Flames slammed into the jungle floor, spreading out as more rushed down from above. The fire leapt onto everything it touched, burning bright blue leaves to black in mere seconds. Land animals were fleeing, small things that Alistair had never seen running past his feet. Huge birds of prey flapped into the air, some of them on fire.

Caesar grunted without moving, then a strange language exited his lips. He'd never spoken it in front of Alistair before, not even when addressing another gigante.

Alistair's HUD relayed that the temperature was increasing rapidly. A third copter let loose its flames, another one in a corner. They were trapping Alistair's group. The fifth and final would be the middle one, ending their endeavor on this planet.

"Caesar, I need to know something quickly because we're all about to fucking die," he said.

The fourth copter let loose, and flames roared in from all directions, a quarter-mile away at best. The temperature was rapidly increasing.

Alistair felt a hot wind coming from almost directly above him. He looked up, the planet's star reflecting off his helmet. The quadcopter's weapon opened from the bottom, and blue flames circled the edge.

Alistair heard another example of the strange language, but this time it wasn't coming from Caesar. He looked down. They had mere seconds. The giant was pointing east with his blade. "*GO!*" Caesar screamed.

Alistair didn't wait. He rushed in the direction the giant told him to, flames roaring in the not-so-distant jungle. He felt the *whoosh* of something from above, his HUD telling him the temperature was rising at a rate it could hardly keep up with.

Warning, incoming fire at your six, it read on the faceplate.

Alistair cut down anything he encountered with his Whip, knowing he had to keep moving forward.

Damage to rear panels, the HUD said as the heat increased. The flames were nearly at his back. Those in front of him were only yards away.

There was nowhere to go.

Then, Alistair found himself falling.

Alistair landed hard on all fours, his Whip clattering in front of him. He leapt forward, grabbed the weapon with his right hand, and rushed to his feet as fast as he could. The Whip spread out, all three lasers ready to kill. His faceplate switched to night vision. Thoreaux was still on all fours, and Caesar had reached a knee.

Another gigante was in front of him, holding a weapon Alistair didn't recognize.

He charged forward, ducking as the giant retreated, then leaping into the air. He kicked out, nailing the creature in the chest before landing on top of him. Alistair thrust his Whip forward, the red lasers floating inches from the gigante's skin. "Who are you?"

The gigante's eyes were wide as he stared at Alistair with fear etched on his face. Alistair could tell he was younger than Caesar, and most likely, he'd never seen anyone or anything move so quickly.

Caesar stepped up behind Alistair. "Don't kill him, boss."

Alistair heard his friend but didn't release the Whip. "Who is he, and how did he know we were out there?" he asked without turning around.

"I have been watching," the fallen gigante said in the same stilted English Caesar used. Alistair could see the fear on his face and watched as wonder slowly crossed it. "What are you?" he asked.

"I shouldn't kill him, Caesar?" Alistair asked.

The giant answered from behind him. "No. He saved us. He'll have knowledge we can use."

Alistair slowly got off the new gigante, although he didn't take his eyes away from him. He took a few steps back, creating space between the two of them before looking at the place they had fallen through. Flames rushed overhead, but they didn't flush down the hole above them. There was nothing but dirt for them to eat, and the rush of the wind wasn't allowing the fire to fill the space they were in.

That much was true—the gigante had saved them from certain death, but for what? He looked across the hole and took the measure of the gigante. He was much younger than Caesar and bigger, which was hard to believe. "Who are you?" Alistair asked.

The gigante cocked his head to the side, and Alistair realized his mistake. The creature had no sense of self-identity, let alone a name.

"Why did you save us?" Alistair asked instead.

The gigante's head was still cocked to the side, and that wonder was still on his face. "I heard how you spoke to the servants."

Alistair looked at Caesar. "What's he talking about?"

"He is an outcast," Caesar answered. "Breeding went wrong. He'll never fit in on the outside because he will not follow like the rest of us. He probably could not follow his clan leader, and that is why he is here, hiding."

"Why's he so much bigger than you?" Thoreaux asked.

"Newer model," Caesar said without emotion.

Alistair still hadn't taken his eyes off the new gigante. "So, during this game you all play, he'll die in it?"

"Yes, he's probably being hunted right now. You get stripes for killing enemies and outcasts. Someone will want a stripe for him."

Alistair knew what Caesar meant by stripes. He'd seen the scars on the giant's biceps, horizontal lines that nearly filled both arms. Caesar had earned a lot of stripes during his institute.

The newcomer had a few stripes but nothing like Caesar's, despite his massive size.

"Will he follow me like you did in the beginning?" Alistair knew the wonder on the creature's face was because he moved even faster right now due to the new armor.

"Where are you going?" the gigante asked.

Alistair smiled about the giant taking him literally. "We want to kill your clan leader. Can you get us near him?"

The gigante's huge eyebrows rose. He was obviously unable to believe what he was hearing. He turned to Caesar and uttered something in the strange language. The HUD tried to decipher it but was unable to. Caesar responded, and without looking at Alistair, told him and Thoreaux, "He doesn't believe us. He thinks we're some kind of plant."

Thoreaux chuckled inside his helmet, drawing a glare from the new giant.

"Can you convince him we're telling the truth?" Alistair asked.

Caesar said something in the strange language and pointed at the flames above. He gestured at the Whip in Alistair's hand, saying something else.

The giant's eyes followed the gesture and didn't move from the laser weapon.

Caesar grew quiet, and the three of them waited. The giant was fearful. He'd saved them but reverted to a primitive fear that they'd been planted here to kill him even though he'd saved them. This world had no mercy for those it birthed. The owners were every bit as cruel as the Commonwealth. Perhaps even more so.

Alistair retracted his Whip and unhooked his helmet from the neckline, then squatted and placed the helmet between his knees. He heard the fire rushing overhead, the sound different now. The quadcopters hadn't stopped. They were going to burn everything in the forest until nothing but skeletons remained.

"I'm not here to kill you," Alistair said. "I'm here to free you. As awful as it sounds, I will have to kill a lot of your kind for that to happen, including your clan leader. In the end, though, your makers are going to die, and no one else will have to go through what you did." He looked up from the helmet. "Will you show me how to get to your leader?"

The giant squatted in front of Alistair. He pointed at him. "You'll kill the leader?"

Alistair nodded.

"And more?" the giant asked.

"As many as it takes."

The giant, at least a third larger than the one on Alistair's left, began laughing. He laughed so hard he fell on his back and placed his hands on his stomach. They rose and fell with his laughter, and Alistair looked at Caesar.

His friend shrugged as he stared at the laughing giant. "He may be mad. I cannot tell yet."

The giant pointed at Alistair without looking up. "I will take you, yes. We will kill them all. Every last one." His laughter, which sounded quite insane, echoed up the hole and was lost in the fire above.

The game had changed since Caesar played it. Not the rules, but the evolution of the players. The "newer models," as Caesar called them, were bigger, stronger, and faster than Caesar's cohort had been. The newcomer was young, barely sixteen years old, and still had more growing to do. The concept of a name was so new to him that he couldn't grasp it. Alistair gave him one just so the other two could keep up.

"Nero?" Alistair asked the other two.

Caesar, of course, had no reference for the name, though Thoreaux did. The mad emperor who'd been accused of burning down part of Rome to make way for a new aesthetic. Not to mention killing his ex-wife after banishing her.

"Could fit," Thoreaux had said with a shrug as the fire

above slowly burned to a halt.

Thus, the newcomer became Nero.

They stayed in the hole, unsure if scans would show the corporation it existed but knowing it was possible. One missile on this little spot would end all their worries for good, but there wasn't anything they could do just yet. The fire was dying, but it would take time for it to cool enough for them to walk above.

They spent the night in the hole, slowly learning about the new gameplay from Nero.

"Did you dig this hole?" Alistair asked. He was lying on the ground, his head propped up on his helmet.

"No," the giant answered. "Found it."

"Who did?"

Nero shrugged. Alistair looked at Caesar, who was lying on the other side of the hole. "The makers probably built it, as they did everything on this planet."

"Then won't they know it's here?" Alistair asked.

"Do you remember every fort you made as a kid?" Caesar responded. "No. They forget what they build over the years. This may have been here for decades. If the makers knew it was here, we would be dead already. Rest easy on that point, Prometheus."

The game, according to Nero, was every bit as ruthless as Alistair had pictured. Nero had been chased out of his clan a few days before and had stumbled upon the hole in a mad rush to avoid death. Alistair thought he'd been lucky not to break anything on the fall, but after looking at the gigante again, he'd realized luck had nothing to do with it. These brutes were built not to break from something as simple as a fall.

Alistair listened as Nero spoke. He wasn't able to communicate as well as Caesar, and the Titan didn't know if that was because of his age, his breeding, or a cultural change. The laughter from earlier was gone. It was much more like speaking to a droid than anything alive.

Nero's clan leader was planning an assault on the rival clan on this part of the planet. According to Nero, it was supposed to take place two days from now and would involve a bit of trickery on the part of his clan. Alistair let the words land on him without interrupting or saying anything. Nero went through the entire plan as he understood it, and Alistair knew it might not all be accurate given what had happened to Nero days after the plan was concocted. He wasn't exactly a beloved member of the clan.

"This is going to be tough," Thoreaux said when Nero had finished.

The sun was starting to peak, this planet having a faster rotation than Earth's.

"That does seem to be the case," Caesar answered him.

"I need a few hours of sleep," Alistair responded. His HUD said the ground above would take another twenty-four hours of cooling off to be ready for them to attempt an escape. He needed time to think. He had nothing to give those who followed him at that moment. Communication with the dreadnought was still being silenced.

They were on their own.

"I'll take first watch," Thoreaux said, though Alistair knew he also needed sleep. Hopefully, they would all get some sleep before they had to climb out of this hole.

Alistair turned over on his side. It took him a while to sleep, and when he did, he saw the future.

CHAPTER FOURTEEN

Alistair knew he was in the dreams of the modified. He didn't know *where*, but he figured out when because he'd never seen any of this before. Thoreaux and Caesar were with him.

Or rather, they were in front of him.

Thoreaux was in his Fire Starter armor, as was Alistair. Caesar was bloody and beaten, on his knees, and staring up at a gigante almost twice his size. Thoreaux had a laser blade in his right hand, and his armor was broken and shredded in places. He looked at a human who stood behind a desk with a strange weapon in his hand. It looked like a MechPulse but wasn't one.

Alistair stood behind them both, a shattered window at his back. Wind whipped past him. As he peered over his shoulder, he realized they were in a skyscraper. He didn't know how they'd gotten here. That hadn't been revealed to him. He turned his head back to the scene in front of him. One of the two was going to die. Alistair couldn't save them both; the distance was too great.

Caesar had somehow been beaten by the monster standing above him, and the human wearing the suit was too far away for Thoreaux to harm.

One would die, and Alistair had to choose which one.

He heard a copter rising from behind, knowing what the sound meant as surely as he knew what the scene in front of him meant. One would die, and if he didn't pick soon, the copter would ensure they all died.

Alistair didn't know who to choose. He didn't know what the final result would be, whether saving one or the other would result in something more or less catastrophic.

There was time. The copter's wind picked up its intensity. Weapons would begin firing soon, chopping them all to pieces.

Alistair knew he was in a dream, but he understood this choice would come to him sooner or later.

He looked down at the floor, seeing shards of glass shaking as the copter's blades grew closer. He couldn't choose between Caesar and Thoreaux. Even if he knew the end result, it was an impossible decision.

Whoosh, whoosh, whoosh.

He felt the wind of the copter's blades against him, and he suddenly heard the sound of their massive shells firing into the room. One exploded against the wall in front of him, another at his feet, sending him flying into the air.

He hit a table, knocking it over, and still shells fired through the open window. He struggled to his feet and watched in horror as a laser blade took off Caesar's head. At nearly the same time, a massive shell caught Thoreaux in the spine, splitting him almost in half.

Alistair stared at the carnage, unable to do anything or stop the death coming for his friends. He had led them here to this strange world, and now they were dead.

He saw the shell coming for him and then—

CHAPTER FIFTEEN

Alistair awoke with a jolt. His right hand had gone to his holstered Whip. He was lying on his side, and his eyes were wide open. He looked at Thoreaux, who was sleeping on his back, his head tilted toward the top of the hole.

What did I just see? he asked himself, feeling real fear. That hadn't been a shared dream, and it wasn't a look into a current state. He'd been shown a glimpse of the future, something that would come.

Alistair didn't understand it, just as he didn't understand much in this modified form. He was a stranger in his own mind and body.

He rolled onto his back. Caesar was asleep on the other side of him, and he saw Nero sitting on the other side of the hole. He sat with his legs crossed beneath him and was staring directly at Alistair.

Alistair knew that if the creature had made any movement toward the three of them, all three would have been ready for war before he could hurt them, so he felt no anger at the other two for sleeping.

Nero motioned for Alistair to join him on the other side. He stood, and Caesar's eyes opened as he did, narrow and looking for danger.

"It's okay," Alistair said.

Caesar watched him walk across the small space and sit down next to the gigante. He stared for some time, but Alistair turned his attention to Nero.

"What did you see?" the giant asked.

"How do you know I saw anything?"

Nero smirked, then pointed two fingers first at his eyes, then at Alistair. The message was simple: *I watched you.*

"What did you see?" he asked again.

"A building," Alistair answered, unsure of why he was answering the giant's question and how the giant knew he'd seen anything. Perhaps it just felt good to tell someone. He wouldn't tell this newcomer everything, but anything was better than nothing. Because Alistair knew the truth. What he'd seen would become reality. They wouldn't die here in this jungle, but at least one of them would meet their end atop some building.

"What did the building look like?" The smirk had disappeared from the giant's face.

Alistair didn't know how to explain it to him. He didn't know what Nero would and wouldn't understand. "It's not like here. There are no jungles, no plants."

"Something the makers made, yes?"

Alistair's eyes widened. The giant understood. "Yes. Exactly."

"Tall?"

Alistair nodded. "Yeah, it was tall."

Nero smiled, and when he did, he looked insane. "You see far, don't you?"

"How do you know that?"

The giant's smiled widened. "I know. We will get there. Do you think you will die when you get there?"

Alistair didn't understand how the giant could know these things. He looked over his shoulder at his friends. Their chests were rising and dropping steadily. He turned back to Nero. "I don't know. Are you able to see far, too?"

"I see enough. I see something is different about you. Now you answer me. Will you die when you get to that building?"

"Why does it matter?" Alistair asked.

Nero cocked his head as if Alistair were insane. "Because I want to live. If you die, I die." He was still smiling. It was as if a split personality lived inside this creature's skull, one that was mad and one that was robotic.

"I don't know," Alistair answered him. "Get some sleep, Nero. I'll keep watch."

The giant nimbly hopped to his feet, the smile fading from his face. "I will get you to the tower. You stay alive," he said as he passed.

***

They pulled themselves out of the pit, and Alistair gazed at the destruction. Life forms of all kinds had been destroyed, burnt to ash to kill him. There were no plants, no animals, nothing but black ash everywhere.

In the distance, Alistair could see evidence of life, plants on the edges of all this death. Smoke rose all around them from smoldering ashes, but it wasn't hot enough to injure the suits or the armor the gigantes wore.

"We need to get out of this area, then find food," Alistair said. They had another twenty-four hours until the gigante assault happened, and that wasn't much time to do anything. He looked at the sky, hoping to see the dreadnought. He saw only the sky. The corporation must have done their scans, found no lifeforms after two days, and left the area.

"Come," Nero said.

The world's star was sinking below the horizon. That would give them some cover. Alistair didn't know where they would get food, only that they'd need it soon if they were to have the strength they required for tomorrow.

They fled the blackened ash, running as fast as they could. None of Alistair's group could keep up with Nero. The giant was too powerful and not weak from lack of sustenance. Caesar wasn't lying with his "new model" comment. As they ran, Alistair wondered how he would fare in the coming fight. Were these creatures too powerful for him to come out on top? Were they all as kooky as the one now leading them, the continued breeding creating burnt fuses inside their heads?

None of the questions could be answered until he saw more of them. Even Alistair's superior body was slowing down as they reached the edge of the burned land.

Nero led them into the wildly colored foliage, stopping about a half-mile in. He turned to look at the three of them and saw that they were all spent. "Wait here," he told them, then bounded into the jungle.

Alistair watched him go, shocked by how easily

someone of his size simply disappeared. Even the noises of his passage faded to nothing in a short time.

Thoreaux stepped up next to Alistair. "You think he's going to get more of them to kill us? Maybe buy his way back into the clan?"

Caesar sat down hard onto the ground. "No. That won't happen. His type is different, even new models. They might create them to teach the rest of us what happens when we refuse to follow those who are stronger than us. He'll never bow to anyone. The only reason he is helping us now is that you didn't try to force him, and he sees it as his only way out." Caesar stretched out on the jungle floor, the neon-yellow and red plants stretching out of his way to avoid danger. "In the end, we will have to kill him. He'll never follow us, not by command or his own volition. His type only does what they want to."

Alistair had never heard Caesar talk in such a way. The giant closed his eyes and placed his hands behind his head. "He won't trade us because he has no one to trade us to. When we've won, I will have to kill him. To set something like him loose in the universe would only create havoc."

Thoreaux turned to Alistair, who shrugged. He didn't understand the strange culture that existed in this even stranger jungle.

He sat down to wait for the giant to return.

Thoreaux leaned against a far tree and let his faceplate retract into the helmet. "So, are you going to tell us what the Hades you two were talking about with that building?"

"I'm wondering the same," Caesar said.

Gods, Alistair thought as he fell back into the foliage. They had been awake and listening. He wasn't going to be able to keep secrets from them as the AllMother had from her followers. "You two don't want to rest and wait for Nero?"

"We can rest while you talk," the giant responded.

Thoreaux laughed and slowly slid down the tree until he was sitting. "Agreed. We rest. You talk."

Alistair sighed. There wasn't any point in lying to them. Holding it back wouldn't help and might hurt in the long run. "You've both heard of the dreams of the modified, right?"

Thoreaux nodded.

"The AllMother told me," Caesar said.

Alistair hadn't seen that coming. "The AllMother did?"

Caesar nodded without opening his eyes. "She said I would need to know in order to help you one day."

Alistair turned to Thoreaux. "She tell you the same?"

His second grinned at him. "You worry about your conversations with the AllMother. I'll worry about mine."

Alistair sighed. He leaned forward, wrapped his arms around his knees, and told them what he'd seen: the building, the destroyed boardroom, the giant, and the man in the suit. He told them how he felt he'd have to choose between them or they all would die. He told them that in the dream, they'd all been cut down.

"And you think it's real?" Thoreaux asked.

Alistair nodded. "I know it is. There's no question about it. Caesar, how did Nero know I was seeing something?"

The giant hadn't said anything during the story, nor had he opened his eyes. At Alistair's question, he did, though. He was silent, only stared at the sky.

"Caesar?"

"This is not good," the giant said without looking around.

"I sorta feel that about your entire home planet, big man," Thoreaux said, "but what's not good about *this* part?"

"He is touched." Caesar brought a finger up to his temple and tapped it.

"Insane?" Alistair asked.

Caesar shook his head. "No. Touched like you, boss. He cannot see as far as you, nor can he do the things you can, but he is touched all the same."

Alistair's face grew concerned. "He's a telepath? He can see the future?" As far as he knew, no one could do that, not until he'd dreamed about it a few days ago. The AllMother had never mentioned the future, only the shared dreams and the ability to see across galaxies. His mind was expanding, and now he was being told another creature had a similar power? "Did you know he was touched, Caesar?"

The giant shook his head. "No. I thought there might be a chance. The touched are rare among us, and every time, they are hunted down and killed, just as he was going to be. The touched cannot follow. They're incapable of it."

"Why didn't you mention this before, Caesar? Why didn't you tell us he was touched when we first met him?"

The giant remained calm. "I couldn't know. Even now, I can't be sure. He might not be touched, just insane. However, if he could tell you were dreaming, I'd venture to say he's probably touched."

Alistair unhooked his helmet from his neckline and placed it on the ground next to him. What was he going to do, tell this giant such a thing wasn't true because he didn't think it was possible?

Allie, his wife asked from her place inside his mind. *Is someone like* you *supposed to exist?*

He knew the answer to that as well.

"I can see how it's possible," Thoreaux said, looking at the sky. "They breed creatures here, but not like we do in our Solar System. There's no mother and father. No procreating. This is all done in a lab, so in a way, they're just another form of the modified. Mutants, as Earth calls them. Truthfully, if they're creating modified humans— which they are since the gigantes' DNA is based on ours— sooner or later they're going to create a modified who has mental abilities. Maybe they do it by mistake, or maybe they do it on purpose. Who knows?"

"Why would they do it on purpose?" Alistair asked.

"To teach the gigante to hunt their own kind, even when they're on the same team." Thoreaux shrugged. "I certainly don't think it's beyond their cruelty to do such a thing."

Alistair ran his hands through his hair. Perhaps it did make sense, in a way that only this strange part of the universe could. Or maybe it made sense from the way Alistair's solar system did. Because humans had created the modified and now they were second-class citizens, sometimes even hunted. So why wouldn't other humans do it all these miles away?

He and I are the same in that way, then, Alistair thought. *He, Caesar, and me. All Modified, just in different ways.*

Alistair heard the steps before anyone else in his group did and bounded to his feet, his Whip unfurled and ready to kill. The footsteps grew louder, whoever was coming doing nothing to hide their approach. The other two were on their feet seconds after Alistair.

The strange language came from the wild-colored forest. "It's him," Caesar said, visibly relaxing.

Nero stepped through purple vines, an animal slung over his right shoulder. The animal had jagged bone-like points across its body, obviously for protection. Its forehead contained an elaborate set of horns, and a tongue lolled from between vicious-looking teeth. It easily weighed two hundred pounds, perhaps more, and looked like a wild cross between a porcupine, a deer, and a wolf, although none of them were Earthborn.

Nero slung the animal down in front of them and smiled from ear to ear. "Eat. Tomorrow we die."

Alistair ate the meat after having watched the two gigantes skin and clean the animal as if they were surgeons. Despite the different modes, they'd both grown up learning how to do this, and they both knew the animal well.

They carved the meat down to the bone and made a small fire to cook it. They did all this quickly and efficiently, then scattered dirt on the fire so it wouldn't be seen. They ate in silence, not out of fear but out of hunger. The meat was gamey and tougher than anything Alistair had experienced before, but he ate it gratefully. Given how hungry he'd been, it might have been the greatest meal of his life.

After they were finished, Alistair looked at the two

moons in the sky. Everyone was quiet and had been since the meal was finished.

Alistair understood what Nero's clan leader was attempting. Tomorrow would be extremely dangerous for his group. In a way, Alistair admired it. The plan was something he might have tried if he'd had the limitations placed on him by this game.

"How far are we from the nests, Nero?" he asked.

"Not far," the giant answered.

Alistair sat up. "I'd like to see them."

Thoreaux followed suit, looking at Alistair. "You think that's a good idea, Pro? The clan will be getting ready to grab the creatures soon."

Alistair climbed to his feet, picking up his helmet. "It's fine. Nero, can you keep us from being seen?"

The gigante was squatting, stretching his quads. "Yes, I should be able to."

Alistair smiled at Thoreaux. "See, everything is fine."

The gigante nodded without looking at either of them. "It is fine. We die tomorrow. Not tonight."

Thoreaux didn't look pleased. "You want us to come, Pro?"

"No, you two stay here. We'll be back shortly. I just want a look at what we'll be going up against tomorrow."

Thoreaux didn't argue, and Caesar remained quiet. Both of them knew that wasn't the only reason he wanted to walk with Nero. They'd just have to trust he could keep himself alive in this strange jungle.

The two started walking. Alistair didn't ask how long it would take, and truthfully, he didn't care. Getting an eye on the creatures was secondary to the conversation he wanted to have. He waited until they were out of earshot of his friends, admiring the way the giant moved through the jungle as if he were a much smaller creature. He stepped lightly and dodged vines in a way Alistair never could.

The giant made no movements that suggested he might try to hurt Alistair. He seemed completely enveloped in moving through the dark forest, his senses alert to everything around him.

Alistair walked a few feet behind him, but the gigante didn't seem nervous about that either. Whether it was him being touched or him simply trusting Alistair was anyone's guess.

"Do you know what touched means, Nero?" he finally asked from behind the giant.

The big creature nodded. "I do."

"Are you touched? Is that how you knew I was dreaming?"

Nero stopped walking, putting Alistair on edge. He didn't turn around but only looked at the ground. "I don't know if I am touched. I see things sometimes. Not all the time. I saw you were dreaming something important, but I didn't know what."

"What else do you see?"

Nero looked into the forest. "I saw the death of my clan leader. I saw you. The other things fade over time. I do not know why."

"You told your clan leader you saw him fall?" Alistair asked.

"No. There was no need. He knew I saw it, so he tried to kill me." Nero laughed, again sounding mad. "I didn't see that coming, though."

"You saw me coming?"

Nero pointed into the sky, his head following his finger. "You floated down by yourself. You had a weapon like the one you have now, and your armor was mostly destroyed, but I saw you coming days before you got here."

Alistair had seen his armor badly damaged too in his dream. He didn't doubt Caesar any longer. Touched or modified, it all came down to the same thing. This gigante had powers different from those on this planet, or at least most of them, and he was hunted for it. Alistair didn't know if the rest of what Caesar had said was true, whether the gigante could never follow anyone, or if he'd have to be killed in the end.

Alistair would have to find that out on his own.

He had one more question to ask. "Can you see what happens tomorrow? Or after?"

"I cannot see as far as your dream. I cannot see to the makers' rooms. I only see death. Rivers of death. You are bringing those rivers, but I do not know if you will be swept up in them as well. The whole planet may be swept away in one red river."

Alistair swallowed, wishing he hadn't asked. "Let's go, Nero. We'll need some sleep before tomorrow, so we should hurry."

The giant nodded and started forward as if nothing had been discussed. They continued through the jungle, Alistair's HUD working similarly to Nero's senses, both constantly relaying any possible dangers to them.

After another hour of hiking, the giant abruptly squatted and motioned for Alistair to do the same at his side.

They'd reached another cliff edge, although Alistair had no idea where it was in relation to the original one they'd nearly died at. He heard no water rushing at the bottom, which hopefully meant none of those murderous eels waited there. Alistair squatted next to Nero and felt the giant carefully lean into his side.

The whisper was nearly noiseless. Alistair had to turn up the volume on his helmet to hear it. "Move to the edge of the cliff. Look down. Make no noise or you will die, spaceman."

Alistair cranked the volume of his voice down to match the giant's. "You're not coming?"

The giant shook his head. "Do not worry. You will not die at my hands if you make too much noise." He smiled, the moon twinkling off his big white teeth and dark-brown eyes.

"Thanks, buddy," Alistair said. He laid on his stomach and slowly crawled forward, his HUD telling him the distance until he reached the edge.

His head crossed the plane from ground to air and he looked down, not sure what to expect.

His mouth opened, and he drew a breath. He turned the night vision down on his helmet, letting the moons' natural glow illuminate the miraculous creatures beneath him.

The beasts below him had wings. Giant birds. That was the first way his brain tried to translate what he saw, yet such primitive words failed. As he lay there watching them, he saw one coming in to land on the massive ledge beneath him. It flew in at high speed, and fifty yards away, it started to slow, its flapping wings sending huge gusts of winds to buffet the rock face.

Alistair saw the creature in full at that moment. It had talons the color of steel. The talons were attached to massive legs covered with feathers like a bird's, but instead of a single pair of legs, there were two, one in front and the other in back.

Alistair could see the muscle rippling beneath its feathers.

The other beasts moved out of its way as it landed with a dead animal hanging from one of its talons. They were night hunters, and Alistair was glad none had taken a liking to him since he saw no way of killing the thing. From beak to tail, it was twenty-five yards long, double the size of the largest creature he'd ever seen. The creature opened its mouth, and where a bird might have tiny teeth if any, this thing had the sharp, pointed teeth of an Earth shark. Alistair understood that the beast would shake its head in giant arcs, and the teeth would cut its enemy to shreds. There was no need to bite or readjust. It only had to shake its head and the teeth would do the rest.

The "nest" beneath him stretched across the entire cliff face. The birds had built it, not the makers. Alistair hadn't believed it possible when Nero first explained it, but now he had no doubt. Their steel-colored beaks had carved out the platform over long years. Alistair might think of them as beasts, but there was intelligence in these animals.

Alistair slowly and quietly crept back to where Nero waited for him.

He said nothing as they turned and left.

Only one thought held firm in his mind. What the giant had told him earlier.

I only see death. Rivers of death.

CHAPTER SIXTEEN

Caesar silently stood from his place on the ground. He'd purposely slept farther away from Alistair and Thoreaux, knowing what he would do tonight. He'd been thinking a lot about what to do, about Alistair's plan.

There were things about this world Alistair and Thoreaux didn't understand. There were creatures here they would never see, some that had eyes on them right now. Caesar knew them—or at least most of them—but some of the makers' creations were beyond what Caesar would know about.

He and Nero both knew of the creatures they would soon come up against. Nero had kept silent about them for the most part, and Caesar had said nothing either.

What Caesar wanted to know was *why* Nero had said so little. He'd only told them of the physical nature of the beasts, but the...

Caesar's thoughts broke off for a moment when the word he wanted eluded his grasp. It was a new word that had been introduced to him since meeting Alistair. Something he was just starting to come to understand beyond intuitively.

Nero hadn't told Alistair of the beasts' "spirituality." Caesar had no idea if the makers knew about this spiritual part of them, and he didn't care. The gigantes knew of it. They envied it because of their brutish lives. They had been given no souls or told they had none so many times that there was very little difference in the end. The beasts they would soon battle weren't like that.

Caesar stood in the darkness. He'd slept near Nero, and the giant was staring at him from his spot on the ground. He raised a finger to his lips, telling the other to be quiet. Nero understood, and he rose silently from the jungle floor.

Alistair was powerful, god-like in some ways. However, on this world, in this jungle, Caesar held the advantage. He and Nero had been born into this mess, and they could move without either human hearing them.

Caesar and Nero walked into the night, neither saying anything. The sounds their steps made were indistinguishable from the rest of the jungle noises.

When they were well out of earshot of the humans, Caesar squatted. Nero squatted too, the giants facing each other.

Caesar spoke in their native tongue, the one that hardly anyone outside of the gigantes knew. Perhaps the makers knew it, although they never spoke it. He asked his question, then stared at Nero. The gigante was touched, whether or not Alistair believed it, and Caesar believed he'd have to be killed in the end. Right now, though, he needed to understand why the touched gigante hadn't told

Alistair more about the animals that would surely try to kill them all.

The moon lit the giant's square face, and Nero looked at the ground. He stuck his finger in it and drew a large circle in the dirt. He said something in their native language, then placed his finger in the dirt five times, creating five dots.

He looked up at Caesar and spoke one more sentence.

He looked back down and scattered four of the five dots, leaving one remaining.

Nero said one more thing and then stood, leaving the circle and the last dot there.

Caesar stared at it for a long time. The two moons continued their rotation, moving closer and closer to the horizon, but he didn't move. He had to make a decision, one he didn't feel comfortable about. He knew he no longer had to follow Prometheus. He could go his own way. He was free; that was something Pro had shown him. He followed the man because he wanted to. In his way, Pro had become a maker, remaking Caesar into something very different from the beast he had first met.

Now Caesar had a choice. Nero had already made his. The gigante was touched, and there wasn't anything Caesar could do to convince him to make a different decision.

Would Caesar tell him of the spiritual nature of these beasts, or would he let Pro walk into it blind?

Caesar understood this was his part in making Prometheus. To come out of this alive would be to come out of it greater than he had ventured into it. To conquer these beasts, he'd have to become more than he currently was.

Would telling Prometheus this hinder or hurt him?

The planet's star was about to rise when Caesar made his decision. He and Pro were very different creatures, the gigante realized. Caesar had needed to be molded by a potter's hand, gently letting him come to realizations.

Prometheus had been and would continue to be molded by a blacksmith's forge. Hard and hot.

For better or worse, Caesar decided to keep silent. He would let the hard and hot jungle and the heat of battle forge what Prometheus would become. Nero was right, and as Caesar stood, he looked at the remaining dot. Everyone else here could die, and the circle would hold. Prometheus held the circle together. Telling him of the future might break him. Pro must meet the future on his own terms and in his own time.

That was how Caesar could help make him.

Binsum Tinsert Immorium Dax woke up before dawn, having no idea what the gigante now named Nero saw for this day. To him, the only bothersome thing was the dreadnought still floating above the planet. They had killed the intruders a few days ago, and the scans had shown no signs of life where the flames had burned.

Bin had transferred as much to the dreadnought, letting them know there was no reason for them to remain. The people they'd sent were dead. Their remains destroyed, burnt to ashes.

The dreadnought still had not moved. It was too far out of the planet's orbit to cause damage but close enough to embark on a landing if it wished. That bothered Bin. He hadn't attacked yet because he still wasn't sure where this dreadnought was from. His corporation's buyers stretched across galaxies. Regardless of the three-man invasion, Bin didn't want to anger possible customers by killing an untold number of people in a so-far-peaceful dreadnought.

He threw his blankets off and stared at the ceiling.

Still, it would have to be dealt with. He was tired of the thing floating above his planet. There were any number of important things to worry about, and he didn't need this added to the mix.

"Alrain," he said to the empty room, waiting for the AI to connect him.

"Yes, Lord Dax?" his head of security said a few seconds later. That was one thing Bin liked about the old man. He was *always* awake before Bin.

"By the end of the day, I want to know where that dreadnought is from, and I want it out of my planet's orbit. Do you understand? I've asked this too many times, and I'm not going to ask again."

"We've nearly tracked down its origin. I'll have it to you by the end of the day."

"Good."

The transmission ended, and Bin swung his feet to the floor. The AI began telling him what he could expect this day, starting with the Battle of the Rocs. Such a battle rarely occurred since it took serious balls by one of the gigantes to try to ride the giant Rocs. Bin's father's head of research had thought the creatures up decades ago, naming them from some forgotten mythical legend from Earth. The rocs truly were majestic creatures. Most of the time, the clan that tried to ride the rocs was chewed to bits and their treasure was appropriated by the remaining clans.

Every once in a while, though, the damned gigantes managed to do it. When they succeeded, prices went up for that group. Bin planned to watch the battle because such a boon to profits would help him forget about the damned dreadnought.

"Ask the rest of the board who is going to watch the battle. Do we have percentages on whether or not the gigantes will be able to capture the rocs?"

The AI answered him. "Fifty percent of your board will be in attendance. The gigantes have a thirty-five percent chance of successfully riding the rocs today."

Bin smiled at that. It was the highest percentage he'd heard in years. If the gigantes managed to mount those damn bird-things, the game was won, and profits would soar.

Pun intended.

Alistair slept without dreams, and he woke to Nero's giant face staring at him.

His other two warriors were cleaning themselves as best they could with giant leaves, something Caesar or Nero must have shown Thoreaux.

Alistair blinked at the huge head.

A smile spread across Nero's lips. "Are you ready to die, spaceman?"

"And to think, I use to wake up next to a beautiful woman," Alistair mumbled. "Now I get you. Why would I ever want to go back to Earth?" He rolled over and pushed to his feet, stretching his arms high once he was standing.

The air around him was crisp, and the star wasn't yet above the horizon. Alistair could smell himself, and he was indeed ripe, but there was no time to get clean. They'd done him the kindness of letting him sleep in, knowing he would lead them into battle today, and every bit of rest he could get would be helpful.

"How much time do we have?"

Caesar tossed the used leaf to the ground. "An hour to get in position. It should take us thirty standard minutes."

"We let you sleep as long as we could," Thoreaux added.

"Much appreciated. Nero, you coming with us?" Alistair asked.

Nero was still squatting. "Yes, of course. We all die together today, or maybe we all live as one. I'm interested to see which."

Alistair didn't know how to respond, just thought the gigante sounded about like he always did—crazy. Alistair put his armor fully on and asked Nero, "They'll strike at dawn, right?"

The giant stood. "Yes. It's their best chance, both for wrangling the rocs and attacking the other clan."

Alistair nodded and turned his attention to the other two. "We'll know in two hours if this is our opening. You two ready?"

"Ready, boss," Caesar said as he attached his chest plate.

Thoreaux's second-to-last piece of armor connected on his arm. Only his helmet remained. "To say I'm tired of this planet would be an understatement. I cannot get off of it quick enough. So yes, I'm ready."

"Good." He extended his arm to Nero and the giant stared at it, unsure of what it meant. "Thank you for everything, Nero. I'm glad to have you going into battle with us."

The giant's eyes slowly rose to Alistair's.

"I trust you," the former Titan said. He didn't know if the gigante had ever heard such a thing before. Certainly not from the makers, and probably not from his kind, either. Alistair knew what Caesar had said would have to happen to Nero, but if he understood anything about this universe, it was that just because the powers that be said something, it didn't make it so.

He saw tears in Nero's eyes. They welled in the deep holes like clear pools. "Thank you." The giant extended his arm in the same way Alistair had. Alistair grabbed it just below the elbow and felt the creature do the same. He felt the unforgiving strength in the giant's hands.

Alistair trusted that strength would be used against the right people today.

The moons still shone, although they were close to the horizon. On the other side of the world, the star was just below where it could be seen. Alistair knelt in the cold mud, looking at a building that could have come directly out of one of the stories he'd read as a child.

It was a castle of old, made of stone and without electricity or any other power source Alistair could see. A moat surrounded the castle, and patrol guards were stationed every fifty yards or so. The castle proper was a big thing, obviously too big for the number of clan members meant to operate it. Alistair thought that was probably another psychological game with the giants. They had to both protect and service the damned building.

Alistair was a quarter-mile away, the HUD in his helmet revealing everything as if he stood right next to it. The patrol guards were every bit as large as Nero, all of them much larger than Caesar. They positively dwarfed him and Thoreaux. Their weapons weren't drawn, whatever they carried. He'd tried to pry that out of Nero, but the giant only said that each clan had been given different weapons and that he hadn't fought this clan before.

Caesar confirmed the truth of that and said the weapons used when he was here would have long ago been done away with.

Alistair touched the armor on his right arm and it retracted, revealing his flesh.

Thoreaux and Caesar both knew what it meant, and neither paused as they followed his lead.

Alistair's faceplate moved inside his helmet. The air was crisp on his skin.

All three drew blades from their sides, keeping their eyes in front of them.

"I do not kill for glory."

The three of them said the words at the same time, their breath fogging in the air before them.

"I do not kill for malice. I kill because it is right. Because if I do not kill, those who seek to harm me and those I love will do so."

The three warriors took their blades and drew blood from their skin. The blood dripped down to the mud beneath them.

They whispered as one, their words as chilling as any Titan to ever repeat the mantra. "I do not fear the enemy. I do not fear death. I only fear living without protecting those I love. I only fear cowardice and hiding from my duty. As this blood flows, so will I. I bleed now so that I will not later. I bleed now so that those who sow harm against me know that blood does not frighten me. I bleed now because it is this blood that will conquer anyone in my path. See it and fear it. See it and die."

Alistair dipped his hand to his bleeding arm, and as he did, he saw Nero doing the same, watching him. Alistair didn't lose focus on the ritual but brought the blood to his face and drew two lines beneath his eyes.

Nero—and the other two—did the same.

Alistair touched his armor and it spread back down his arm, the faceplate coming down to shield him again.

The star cracked the horizon, sending gold and orange bleeding across the world.

The cries of the rocs reverberated through the air at almost the same time.

"They did it," Caesar whispered. "They fly now."

The rocs cried out again, louder this time, and their sound was one of the fiercest things Alistair had ever heard in his life. There was no fear in the animals' sounds, and their voices carried across the land before they could be seen.

Alistair looked at the patrol units. They'd frozen, clearly understanding what was coming their way. After the third cry from the unseen animals, still hidden in the darkness somehow, one of the units raised a trumpet to their lips as if it were necessary. As if everyone inside that castle hadn't heard the primordial screeches of certain death.

More trumpets seized the air. Candles were lit inside the castle, and from a quarter-mile away, Alistair could hear the sounds of war coming to life. Even on this distant planet, he understood that sound.

The other inside him—the warrior who sang death like bards sang songs—stepped forth.

Prometheus had arrived.

He rushed out of the brush that hid him.

The star rose on their right, and the warrior went to war.

Prometheus saw the first roc. It must have been flying close to the tree line because it shot straight up into the air, and with a force Prometheus could only imagine, streaked toward a sentry.

Its massive beak opened, revealing those horrific teeth. The giant was split in half. The roc rose into the air again, opening its mouth and letting the top half of the giant fall to the ground.

Pro had stopped running without realizing it. The top half of the body hit the muddy ground.

Prometheus broke his trance and took off again.

They had to cross the moat before the battle began in earnest.

Bin was wide awake, and the scent of the coffee beans that had been transported from Earth brewing behind him filled the air. He and half his board floated above the castle, staring down at the starting battle.

Bin was in awe at the rocs. He'd seen them before but never seen them ridden. His father had been a genius to think up a creature like this, then to create one who could wrangle the rocs to do their bidding. No human could ever ride one of those beasts. They would be ripped apart before stepping within ten yards of them.

Bin and his cohort rode in a transport that masqueraded as a cloud. There were no worries about anyone below seeing them. The brutes were far too simplistic to think of such a thing. More, if they were seen, what would it matter?

"Sir," a servant said from behind Bin.

He stuck his hand out without turning around, and the cup of hot coffee was placed in it. He didn't want to be interrupted during this. Such a massacre wouldn't be seen again for a long time, and images from this transport would be spliced together when the promotional videos started going out to the armies and warlords.

Today was a glorious day where money would be made.

"Sir?"

That wasn't one of the servants but one of his board members sitting at the table behind him. Bin preferred, at least at this point, to stand and look through the panels beneath his feet to get an overhead view. Perhaps later, he'd sit and the table and let the holovid show him different angles.

"Bin?" the voice asked.

"For the gods' sakes," Bin said, turning around and

sloshing his coffee. "What in the hell do you want? Can't you let me watch this in peace?"

No one at the table was looking at him. His anger didn't matter in the slightest, which only angered him more.

"Bin, sir, you need to take a look at this."

"Son-of-a-fucking-bitch!" he cursed and stalked to the table. He slammed his coffee down, spilling some over the cup's lip to show how angry he was.

He forgot about that when he looked at the holovid.

The man he'd burnt to a crisp was alive and rushing toward the coming battle.

He wasn't slowing down for the moat, either. Rather, he appeared to be about to attempt to jump it.

"What in the gods' name is happening?" someone whispered.

Bin forgot about his coffee, his rage, and the battle. His eyes focused on the man who was about to attempt the impossible.

Just before Prometheus reached the edge of the moat, he regretted his decision. It was daring, unlikely to be challenged, and would almost surely kill him.

It was far too late to stop the charge, though.

He was rushing forward at top speed. Each time his foot slammed on the ground, it propelled him forward another ten yards. The moat was close, another two jumps away.

Everyone else had slowed and was coming to a stop at the edge of the ravine.

Prometheus kicked off hard, having no idea if he was going to make it across. He propelled himself into the air and went higher and higher, his legs moving as if he were still running. He glanced down and saw those eel creatures beneath. They churned up a frothy storm in the water, sensing something above.

Pro's arc peaked, and he started his descent. It was going to be close. He heard the sound of rocs echoing off the castle walls. He had no idea if they were zeroing in on him. Perhaps he would be plucked from the air and savaged above the toothy beasts in the water.

His HUD showed him distance and time. **Three seconds until impact.**

Two...

One...

Prometheus tucked and rolled, clearing the distance by a single yard.

He rose from the roll with his Whip unleashed and cut down the first giant he saw. The three lasers cut him in quarters. The gigante remained standing for a brief moment, then fell to the ground in four pieces as Pro turned to look at the three on the other side of the moat.

Mayhem reared its confusing head all around him, with gigantes rushing from the castle's doors as others were dropped from the air, the rocs obeying their new masters. The drawbridge was up, one of three that surrounded the castle, and they had made the rocs so necessary. Prometheus needed it to do what came next.

He ran toward the drawbridge. A sentry stood in front of it, a creature wearing black armor who stood three feet taller than him. His head was turned to the sky and he watched the taloned beasts fly to and fro, most likely hoping one didn't spot him.

He dropped his eyes to the man in front of him too late.

Prometheus impaled him without so much as a glance. He ripped his Whip free from the giant's chest while his mind figured out the drawbridge's mechanism. He couldn't see his friends on the other side since the bridge's deck was in his way, but he trusted they were in the right spot. The bridge, like everything else to do with this castle, was something from ancient times. Simple metal and rope.

Prometheus cut through the rope on his right with a single swipe, then moved to the left. The bridge was straining, the metal cogs wanting to turn. He sliced through the second batch of ropes and waited...

Nothing happened.

He heard the footsteps before he saw the person and ducked, slicing his Whip backward at the same time. It hit home, and Prometheus felt the giant drop.

Still the bridge stood.

Prometheus almost cut his own throat when he saw the problem. A metal pole had been stuck between the cogs for something just like this. Two of the three drawbridges were only for emergency escapes. Ropes held them up; there was no mechanizing gear to lower or raise them. The gigantes had done something very wise or very stupid. They had shoved a pipe into it, which Prometheus had missed in his rush.

The drawbridge held firm. Prometheus would have to somehow wrench the pipe free.

Even with the Fire Starter armor, he didn't see how that would be possible.

He rushed to the cogs and gripped the piece of pipe that was visible. He pulled until his shoulder joints creaked, but it wouldn't come free.

Pro turned to look at the battle. Fire was blazing from one of the castle's rooms. The cries and grunts of war were all around him, and the plan he'd worked out was failing.

***

"He's a godsdamn fool," Bin said with a chuckle.

The former Titan was pulling on a simple tool the gigantes had used for decades to stop drawbridge invasions, a metal pipe in the cogs that they hoped invaders wouldn't think about when cutting the ropes.

"He's cut off from his reinforcements. He doesn't have a fucking chance."

Bin had been nervous minutes before, watching the man clear a span that should've been impossible. He'd cut down three gigantes as if he'd somehow known where they would move before it happened, his movements as fluid as water.

Now, though, he was finished. It didn't matter how fast or strong he was. One man against rocs and gigantes? Soon he'd just be another body lying on the battlefield.

"Sir," someone said but didn't finish.

They didn't need to because Bin saw what was happening, and words couldn't describe it.

***

Prometheus knew he needed his friends, human and gigante, if any chance was to be had on this side.

He also knew he wasn't physically strong enough to do what was needed. Perhaps no one in the universe was, or perhaps everyone but him. All he knew was that he couldn't shift that pipe, and there wasn't time to make his way to the second drawbridge.

Prometheus had to summon the thing he didn't understand, the power granted him by an old woman without his consent. The thing that let him see the future and travel to other parts of the galaxy.

For the first time since he'd been modified, he had to get some control over it or perish.

Prometheus shut his Whip down and holstered it.

He turned so that his back was to the battle and he faced the unmoving cog.

Pro closed his eyes and thought he would have to turn the sound on his helmet down. However, the moment he saw blackness, he heard nothing. It was as if he'd walked into a sound- and sight-proof room.

His eyes flashed open, and sound immediately returned.

Hurry now, Allie, his wife whispered from her special place in his mind. *You must gain control, or all is lost.*

Prometheus closed his eyes, and once again, the battle sounds ceased. He was alone. In the darkness of his mind, nothing could get in. Here, and if only for now, he was at peace.

The pipe appeared in the darkness, although not as it had looked when his eyes were open. Everything was black and white, as if drawn in ash on white paper.

Pro reached out with his mind, an odd feeling he didn't know how to describe even to himself. However, he did it as ruthlessly as he would fight with his Whip against an enemy.

He blanketed himself over the pipe. They were the only two things inside his mind: him and that pipe.

Suddenly the white color turned a liquid red, and Pro knew what had happened.

His eyes opened wide again, and the drawbridge was falling. He glanced at the cog spinning wildly fast on his right, the melted pipe still red-hot inside the gears, which had been completely dismantled.

The drawbridge landed on the other side, and the other three started their mad dash across.

There you go, Allie, Luna said, and her voice surely would have included a smile if she stood in front of him. *Now all you have to do is conquer two clans of giants and some wild bird creatures.*

Pro couldn't help but smile at the sarcastic version of Luna his mind projected. Gods, he loved her.

The giants made it first. Thoreaux was close behind.

They stared at the battle.

"Same plan?" Thoreaux asked.

"Of course," Prometheus responded. "Things are going splendidly so far."

"You meant to take that long on the drawbridge, did you?" Thoreaux pulled the MechPulse off his back.

"Oh, yeah," Alistair said. "All part of the plan. Let's go."

Nero's grin was wild, and he had a laser blade in each hand. "Yes. We probably should not take any more rests, spaceman."

"What the fuck was that?" Bin screamed. "Someone tell me right now! What the *fuck* was that?"

Everyone at the table was silent. No one looked at Bin. They had all seen something impossible. Not impossible, as in a man making an unreal leap or cutting down gigantes like stalks of corn.

They stared at something that even the touched gigantes couldn't hope to do.

"AI," Bin snarled, "tell me what I just saw. What did that man just do?"

"I am not able to, Lord Dax," the AI responded, sounding positively perplexed.

Bin knew what his brain was saying he'd seen.

The former Titan had turned and faced the drawbridge. He'd stood there for five or ten seconds, then the metal pipe sticking out of the cog had melted.

It had turned red, then for a brief instant, white-hot, then the cog had turned, the weight of the drawbridge too much, and the once-cold steel of the pipe was ripped apart.

"Replay it," Bin commanded. "Show it to me again and zero in on the Titan's armor."

There had to be some kind of weapon. They must have missed something because nothing else was possible.

The AI did as it was told, slowing down the replay. As it showed the board members again, it said, "I've rerun the scene ten thousand times since it happened. There is no detectable weapon involved, Lord Dax."

What in Hades do I do? Bin wondered. "Can we turn the gigantes' focus on the intruders?"

"Sir, with all due respect, there's no way to turn anything right now. This is the Battle of the Rocs."

Bin whirled on the woman. "I know what the fuck it is. Is there anything we can do about these godsdamn intruders walking into our company?"

Tinkerman, a usually quiet mustachioed man, leaned back in his chair and said very calmly, "I believe they may be doing something about it themselves right now." He pointed at the holovid in the middle of the table.

CHAPTER SEVENTEEN

Dead bodies lay strewn around the castle's main entrance. The gigantes inside had tried to close the gate, but the roc had eaten them like berries picked from plants. The roc could have gone through the entrance, but the creature was intelligent enough to know it was too big to be effective inside. Instead, it guarded the entrance, somehow knowing which gigante to let in and which to kill.

Prometheus didn't have a damn clue how it knew. Maybe the fucking birds were as touched as Nero, but at least fifty dead laid next to it, and more gigante kept running beneath his massive wings to fill the castle.

This battle was a massacre, a rout, and the mayhem that had once enveloped the area was quickly becoming a one-sided victory. Then the remaining clan's might could focus on Prometheus and his crew.

The roc caught a glimpse of him, bent forward on its front talons, and screeched. Wind rushed around Prometheus, the air from the beast's lungs impressive by itself. Blood ran down its hard beak, and flesh hung from its teeth.

"Is this the one?" Prometheus screamed.

Nero cut through a gigante smaller than him about five yards from Pro. He looked over his shoulder and shouted back, oddly cool for all the death around him, "Unfortunately, no!"

The other three were keeping the horde at bay, but it wouldn't last much longer. Prometheus knew what they had to do, and this godsdamn bird was in his way.

There wasn't time to plan out a battle. The roc looked angry. Each of its eyes was almost as big as Prometheus. It scratched at the stony ground as if daring the small man to try to get past it.

The creature was intelligent. It didn't walk out to attack Pro but remained at the gate, knowing that to give up its position could be disastrous.

Gods be with me, Prometheus prayed silently. It was a foolish thing for him to do, but he knew of no other way to get around this creature besides divine intervention.

He started forward, not letting his armor propel him too high. He wanted to remain close to the ground for this attack.

The creature shrieked again, baring its razor-like teeth at him.

Finally, when he was a few yards from it, the roc stepped forth, one massive talon raised and its beak open, ready to rip Prometheus to shreds.

He dropped his feet and slid forward. Sparks flew around him as his metal armor scraped across the stone. He grabbed his Whip's hilt with both hands, flicking it out as far as it would go into the air and forming a straight line.

A scream filled his helmet, one that sounded as if a god were dying. Prometheus was still skidding across the stone as blood and intestines fell on him.

He reached the tail of the bird, thrust his foot down, and stood up, spinning in case the creature was still ready to battle.

Prometheus watched from behind the roc. It staggered as it tried to turn around, as if the contents of its body weren't spreading out across the stone beneath it.

The creature collapsed, and the great cry ended.

Those still in the courtyard paused to stare at the dead roc.

That was when the trouble started for Prometheus.

Bin's anger had faded. His disbelief was gone.

His father had taught him well of the gods. The Earthborn, if they believed at all, thought them beings who wound up this universe and then gallivanted away to their own homes in some parallel universe. The Earthborn could have cared less about the gods, thinking themselves the masters of this universe.

Bin knew better.

His father had taught him the truth. Humanity was but a speck that could be wiped out with a universal sneeze. It was important to know the gods and to respect them, for one day, humanity might need to call on them.

Perhaps if they were respected, they would answer. Perhaps not. Either way, it was always best to respect them.

Standing in a transport disguised as a cloud, Bin finally realized what he was looking at.

A god.

One transferred from the parallel universe, come here to show humanity what it meant to do battle. Bin realized this as the god cut down a roc, something that had never been done. The rocs died of old age, nothing else, not even in battle, but one was spread out in front of the ancient castle's gate, and the god was drenched in blood and guts.

Bin knew more than that it was a god. He knew which one. He was his father's son, and anything less would be unacceptable.

This was Me'et. Death personified, the very consequence of war.

"What do we do?" Bin asked as the god and his cohort rushed through the castle's gates. Those still standing on the ground did not follow, unable to believe what they'd just witnessed. Bin desperately looked around the table. No one, not a fucking one of his board members was looking back at him.

"I think, sir, it may be time to return home. Let them fight out here. We can deal with the aftermath."

Bin knew the truth, though he couldn't say it aloud. There wasn't any hiding from this god. Me'et had arrived, and death knew no boundaries. Here, there, it would come for them.

All he managed to get out, though, was, "Okay. Get us back to the office."

The two gigantes cranked the gates closed, one on either side tugging at the metal contraptions that would keep out the rest of the gigantes. Prometheus and Thoreaux cut down the giants in the great hall, then Pro took his helmet off and tossed it on the floor.

Blood and intestines covered the faceplate. It was impossible to see through.

"What was that?" he asked as he turned to find Nero. The entry hall was quiet and empty. Pro didn't know where the gigantes who'd flooded inside the gates were. For now, he didn't care.

Sweat poured down Nero's face as he leaned against the closed gate. His wild smile covered his face, and madness danced in his eyes. "I told you death was coming, space-man. Me, you, or the rocs, who can say?"

Pro crossed the room in two steps, stopping in front of Nero. His anger nearly boiled over, but he kept his Whip at his side, its deadly tentacles sensing his nerves. "The rocs. What just happened?"

It was Caesar who spoke from the other side of the gate. "You killed one of theirs, boss. It has never been done before."

Pro's head whipped to the left. "Come again?"

"It's never been done. Now they're coming to kill you."

Prometheus paused, unable to find a single word.

Those who walked the ground had all stopped fighting at the sight of a fallen roc. It was as if those who had lived inside the castle understood they would die once the rocs descended. Like they all had known there was no way to win, but they fought because they were meant to. When they saw one fall, they couldn't believe it, and the battle had stopped.

That was for those on the ground. Those who flew?

The shrieks had come from the entire sky, as if every one of the rocs had been killed instead of one. Prometheus had turned his eyes upward, and the flock that had allowed themselves to be ridden, to be controlled, ceased. They somehow *knew* one of theirs had died, and they'd turned to the gate.

Even now, Prometheus heard them outside, shrieking their death threats at him as if daring him to step outside and face them once more.

"Neither of you knew that would happen?" Prometheus looked at the two gigantes.

They looked as dumbfounded as he felt.

"How could we?" Caesar asked.

Prometheus heard footsteps coming down the twin staircase leading out of the castle's entryway. He turned to see giants standing on the first landing.

A group of ten were kneeling shoulder to shoulder. Their heads were bowed and their weapons were in front of them.

Nero stepped up next to Prometheus. "The one in the middle is the second most powerful in my clan."

Pro looked at Caesar.

The giant nodded. "They serve you now."

Prometheus' eyes traveled up the double staircase. As far as he could see, gigantes bowed in front of him. They had seen or heard about what he'd done to the roc. He was the strongest being they'd ever seen, and they'd been bred or taught to bow at times like this.

As long as he had that strength, they were going to serve him, or at least until he could convince them they were free.

"We serve," came a baritone voice from the middle of the stairs.

"Stand," Prometheus said. He raised a hand and pointed at Thoreaux. "Listen to him for now." Turning to his second, he said, "Look, get them cleared off the stairwell. I've got to figure out what the fuck to do."

Nothing had changed just because the gigantes saw him kill the roc. Or at least, nothing good. He still had to deal with the giant damn birds outside the gate who were screaming at him and mourning their dead.

He ran his armored hand through his hair, forgetting about the blood he spread through it. The plan had been to get on the lead roc, thus killing the head gigante and capturing the bird at the same time. The rocs were built or made or whatever so they would serve a rider who could conquer them, the same as the gigantes. Apparently, no one had ever killed one of these creatures.

Now one was dead, and getting atop the roc leader was seeming like a pretty far-fetched idea, given that they all wanted to kill him.

"Caesar, Nero, what do you think happened to the clan leader? The one that would have been riding the lead roc?"

The gigantes were almost no help. They had never seen anything like this. It was clear now that the reason they'd never mentioned the killing of a roc was that they'd never imagined it. To them, it would have been as strange as not serving a master, at least before Pro had met Caesar. It wasn't possible.

The horde of giants was moving off the staircase now, filing into the entrance.

Something huge banged into the gate, testing the metal bar lying across the inside of it. Pro knew the rocs could physically fit in here, at least some of them. If they got in, they'd lay waste to everyone, including him. What he didn't know was if the bar was going to hold up to the attack or if the door would collapse under the barrage.

Eventually, it's going to collapse, Allie, his wife said without any humor. *You know that. You underestimated these animals, and they don't seem ready to forgive the slaying of one of their own.*

Alistair squatted and closed his eyes, seeing Luna's face. "I don't know what to do," he whispered.

He couldn't kill them all.

They were strange beasts, more terrifying than any army he'd faced. But without the ability to fly...

Pro shook the thought off. It'd been Alistair thinking, but when he stopped, the warrior returned.

"Thoreaux, I'm going to the spire. You all hold the door as long as you can. I imagine these creatures will know once I'm up there, and you won't have to worry."

Thoreaux raised his eyebrows. "You know what you're doing? Because I sure as hell have no idea."

"We're going to find out." He left his helmet on the floor, and with his Whip in hand, he climbed the steps leading to the highest spot this castle had to offer. There he would see what these beasts were about.

Caesar watched Prometheus run up the stairs, his boots echoing on the stone. He moved upward, disappearing as the stairs took him higher. Caesar watched as the gigantes still on the stairs bowed as he passed them.

Prometheus showed no fear, a stoic warrior.

Caesar swallowed, wondering if his choice had been the right one. Of course he and Nero had known what would happen if he slaughtered one of the rocs. That was something the gigante were taught as children since killing one of those creatures would end an entire clan. They were vengeful, *intelligent* animals that would hunt their murderers until the end of time.

That was why it didn't happen. Not because they were too strong or mighty, but because the gigante were not idiots.

Nero came up next to Caesar. "We made the right choice. He will hold here, or he will die. This circle is his, not ours."

Thoreaux was peering at them from across the room, ignoring the docile gigantes for now. He knew as well as everyone else that the game was over for these creatures. They all knew they wouldn't find anyone stronger in this jungle, so there was no more need to fight each other. They would listen until Prometheus fell.

Thoreaux crossed the space between them. "Do you two know what's going to happen up there?"

Caesar opened his mouth to speak, but Nero beat him to it.

"Now he decides how great he is," the giant answered. "That's all we know."

For Caesar as well, that was the truth of the matter.

In the end, Alistair had made a simple decision.

Only he could get them out of this mess. It was he who'd decided to come to this planet. He who'd decided to attack this day. He who had killed the beautiful creature.

Now it was he these rocs wanted, so it was he they would have.

If they could take him. Prometheus stalked upward, not tiring, his body a precision-made machine that neither needed nor wanted rest. He wanted battle. He wanted freedom for his friends below and for those newcomers who had just pledged their lives to him. He could command every one of those gigantes to go outside and throw themselves against the rocs. He could watch as they all died, and in the end, it would only buy him time.

He reached the spire and circled up it, heading to the very top. His plan had been to conquer the warrior who had conquered the lead roc. He would kill the clan leader, ensuring him a new clan's fealty. Then with the rocs in tow, he'd intended to march from clan to clan until they were united.

Then he would go to the corporation's main city and lay waste to it.

A daring plan, and one that hopefully would have had some support from the dreadnought above. All that was dashed now.

The rocs would not be controlled by him or those who had ridden them. Perhaps to them, this had been a game too, one in which they let the toy soldiers ride on their backs if they could wrangle them. When one of theirs died, though, all that had ended.

Prometheus stood at the top of the spire, a small room with a balcony on the far side. The balcony had no banister. One walked out at one's own risk.

He heard the shrieks of the rocs. They weren't at the gate below anymore but had somehow followed him up here.

How, Allie? his wife asked.

He didn't know. Had they seen him in the spire's windows, watched him moving up here, and followed rather than batter themselves against the gates below?

Prometheus unfurled his Whip, letting it fall nearly to the floor.

He stepped to the very edge of the room, beyond which was the balcony.

A roc rose in the distance, its huge wings flapping and bringing it higher. It rose with a power and majesty that could not be duplicated by human hands. No machine could ever look as grand as the animal before him.

Upward it rose, shrieking hate at him. Others flew through the sky, their caws impossibly loud, but they didn't venture to the spire.

This was the leader, and the gigante who had ridden

him most likely no longer lived. These creatures weren't meant to be ridden, and the game was over.

"What are you?" Prometheus whispered.

The transport was nearly back at the city. Bin sat at the conference table, his hands shaking, no coffee in sight. He and the rest of his board stared at the holovid that rose on the table.

Me'et, the god who had come to this universe, had climbed to the top of the castle's spire. Bin could see him, standing in red armor of some kind, his bright red Whip at his side. Blood was smeared on his face, and his hair was full of guts.

The rocs were flying around the castle, screaming at the man who had killed one of their nest.

The head designer was on the transport. He'd had little to say during the past week. The invasion had nothing to do with him; it had been a security breach. However, Bin wanted answers. He still hadn't dared tell this group what he thought. What he *knew*.

None of them would make it out of this alive.

"I need to know what the fuck is going on, Rovan." Bin's hands were shaking, and he was doing everything in his power to keep the tremor out of his voice. "What are those fucking birds programmed to do?"

"Programmed is the wrong word, sir," the head designer responded. "They're flesh and blood, not mach—"

"*I DON'T GIVE A FUCK WHAT YOU CALL IT! WHAT ARE THEY DOING RIGHT NOW?*"

It was clear Rovan was trying to figure out how to describe it in terms Bin could understand. Bin never concerned himself with the actual designs, as long as the prices charged for gigantes continued to rise year after year.

"The gigantes are bred not to have in-group relationships. That's why there are only males. There is no mating. No offspring. They are bred to serve an outer god, and everything else is little more than noise to them. The rocs are very different. Everything is in-group relationships to them. They live very long lives in one area and have offspring throughout their lives. We purposely bred them so their offspring were closer to mammals than reptiles or birds because we wanted that attachment. It was to teach the gigantes the lesson that groups will seek vengeance so that when it happens in the real world, they'll understand it."

He paused and pointed at the roc rising into the sky.

"*That* is what you're witnessing. That roc there, you can think of her as the queen. One of her children was just killed, and now she's going to get her vengeance. This might be the best thing that could have happened."

The man was an idiot. "What happens if he kills the roc?" Bin asked.

Rovan shook his head. "That won't happen."

"What if it *does*?" Bin was trying to keep from shouting, but these morons were making it very hard.

The head designer shrugged and leaned back in his chair. "If he kills the queen, they'll all descend on him. Either way, he's dead. This little insurrection or whatever he was hoping for ended the moment he killed the roc at the bottom of the castle. He's dead."

The transport landed on top of the building, and Bin got off without looking at anyone. He was nearly stumbling as he made his way to the office on the top floor of the corporation's headquarters.

He didn't look around once inside, just found his way to the bathroom. In reality, the room was better than most people had on Earth. It had a full shower, a separate tub, and a toilet in its own smaller room. Bin ignored all that as he leaned on the sink and splashed his face with water.

They were all going to die. He had to get off the planet.

He splashed cold water on his face again, trying to figure out *how* he would get away. The board would throw a collective temper tantrum if he mentioned it since none of them thought this revolution had a chance.

Only Bin knew better. Me'et had arrived.

The voice that spoke sounded like stone scraping stone. "You're a real pussy. You know that, don't you?"

Bin froze, the water running into the porcelain sink the only noise in the office. His eyes flashed to the mirror in front of him. His father was sitting at the desk in the main room.

Bin opened his mouth to speak, but nothing came out.

"They started bringing me out of my sleep the moment the little bullet ship landed," his father said without looking up. He was staring at something on a DataTrack like he'd always done before he went into the deep sleep, the cryogenically frozen state he'd been in for the past few years.

The plan had been... Well, it didn't matter what that plan had been because Bin's damn father was sitting in front of him now. Unfrozen. Not asleep. Alive and sounding as hard as ever.

Bin forgot to turn the water off as he moved from the sink to the bathroom door. He stopped before entering the office. "Me'et is here, Father. He's nearly at our doors."

The old man laughed and cut off his son's words. "You and the gods. You did take that shit to heart, didn't you? Everything I taught you as a boy." He finally looked up from the DataTrack at the doorway. "Tell me, do you really think a god has crossed the dimensions to attack you?"

"I-I..." Bin paused, realizing he couldn't string a sentence together. He swallowed. "You haven't seen him."

The old man waved away the comment and looked back down at the desk. "I've been watching him the same as you have. I just haven't been making up stories and freaking out. I've been preparing for him since the board decided to wake me."

Bin didn't need to ask who'd woken him or what their reasoning had been. Not right now. He didn't know what all this meant for him or the corporation. At that moment, Bin only cared about living. "We need to leave, Father."

The old man slowly shook his head while rolling his eyes. "We're not going anywhere. I'm not abandoning my life's work because a single Titan decided to come to this planet. You'll be there at the end when I kill him." He sighed. "I knew it was too early to leave you with all this. I knew you weren't ready."

He stood up and leaned against the table.

Bin remained in the bathroom, not ready to venture out.

"It doesn't matter," his father continued. "I'm taking over from here on out, and all you need to do, sensitive son of mine, is listen when I say something. I'll kill this little Titan from Earth, and I'll make sure *no one* ever thinks they can take what's mine again."

CHAPTER EIGHTEEN

Prometheus stood with his Whip at his side. The roc was more than thirty yards higher than the spire, about a quarter-mile off. It gave one last shriek and started its descent toward Pro.

The animal flew through the air, its speed increasing each quarter-second as its powerful wings propelled the beast forward.

Pro saw quickly what was going to happen. He retracted his Whip and holstered it. The creature was maybe fifty yards off. It banked right, then curved left again.

Its beak was aimed directly at Prometheus, and its eyes, large and cruel, showed no mercy.

The roc reached the man and its beak opened wide before crushing down, trying its best to trap Prometheus between its wicked teeth. Pro leapt, both hands reaching for the beak's edge as his body collided with the large creature's head. His right hand found purchase as the two took flight. The roc shrieked in anger at having missed its prize, and both were now flying, Pro's left hand and body flapping between the beast's eyes.

It snapped its beak repeatedly, trying to shake the human off its head, but Pro kept holding on as he tried to grip something—anything—with his left hand.

The roc's wings beat hard, thrusting it higher into the air. Prometheus looked down and saw the ground falling away. He turned back, both gravity's pressure and the bird's speed trying to break his grip. The armor helped some, but his body was flopping against the bird's head.

As they soared higher, he regretted not wearing the helmet. He needed to know the suit's integrity, especially the right hand. The beak repeatedly clamped down on it, and though the teeth couldn't get at him, he knew damage was being done.

He needed his right hand almost as much as he needed his head, especially over the next few minutes. When the battle finally came, his left would not be able to handle the Whip as agilely as his right.

The beak opened, and Pro released his grip.

The roc felt it and thrust its wings harder, pushing itself faster and higher.

Pro tumbled toward the ground, slamming into the roc's skull first, then hitting its back. He scrambled to grab something, knowing that if he missed, he was dead.

His left hand grabbed feathers. That slowed his slide down for a moment, enough for his right hand to do the same. The roc screamed as it understood he wasn't falling but had attached himself. It turned, shifting its body from moving toward the sun to the ground.

Its speed increased, gravity plus the roc's momentum propelling the duo downward. Pro thrust himself as hard as he could against the creature. The feathers were rough against his face, and the smells of dirt and nature were strong in his nose. He closed his eyes, letting the wind rush over his back.

He knew what was coming. Survival was a dim hope.

When he felt the roc shift slightly, he looked up. He couldn't tell how far away the ground was, but the animal was only going to slow enough to not kill itself. No amount of strength in the world was going to keep Alistair clinging to the creature.

Another flap of the wings and the bird-like beast was nearly in landing position. Pro thrust his knees up under him, kneeling on the roc.

Three...

Two...

One.

The roc's talons touched down, gripping the dirt. It was moving far too fast even for itself and it lunged forward, unable to find purchase on the ground. It gripped again and was able to jerk to a stop.

Its feathers ripped out of its back, and Pro tumbled over the head.

He hit the ground hard, but he'd tucked enough and somersaulted, once, twice, then found himself skidding on his stomach over brambles and dirt and twisted roots.

His left hand scrambled to slow him while his right held onto the still-holstered Whip. He couldn't lose that at any cost.

Rocks scratched at his bare face, and he kept his eyes

clenched shut. He felt skin ripping off, but he knew he was slowing.

His left hand shoved the ground, throwing him into the air. He opened his eyes and saw the roc coming for him, the talons of the long-legged creature splayed while its powerful wings kept the bird just off the dirt.

Pro's Whip lit the air in front of him, and his feet touched down. The leading talons stretched out for him and he spun to his right as one of the steel-like claws ripped through his armor and flesh, cutting just beneath the ribcage.

The Whip slashed and cut into the roc's wing as Pro slipped to the side.

The creature shrieked as its talons hit the ground.

It slowly turned to face its enemy. The two were both bloodied and battered.

The other rocs were landing now, circling them. The gate of the castle had opened, and men and gigante were flowing out.

Prometheus saw it all, and at the same time, none of it. All that mattered was the creature in front of him.

Its talons scratched the ground, pulling up huge chunks of dirt and roots before tossing them behind it. The roc stretched forward and let out a ferocious shriek.

Pro twirled the Whip with his right hand. The weapon whistled through the air, its three strands barely visible with the speed.

Will it be death, then, Allie? Luna whispered.

Caesar stood between Nero and Thoreaux. None dared enter the circle.

Caesar heard the roc shriek its warning. He saw blood dripping from its wing. He heard the Whip's whistle and watched red liquid leak from his leader.

Would Prometheus get it? Would he finally understand what he'd come here for? Or would they all die in a few moments?

This was why Caesar had chosen to say nothing—because life was the blacksmith for Prometheus. It would either form a sharp blade or break the melting metal.

No.

The Whip slowed in Prometheus' hand.

This wasn't the way.

The Whip's twirl stopped, and the three strands dropped toward the ground.

You don't have to kill the universe to win. You don't have to be the Commonwealth.

The Whip furled back into its hilt. Prometheus stepped back in the dual mind and Alistair came forward.

He looked to his left, then his right. The roc in front of him had paused as if unsure of what was happening. Alistair felt blood dripping from his side, from his face. Every part of him ached.

He turned back to the creature in front of him. A beautiful thing, far more majestic than any human could ever hope to be.

Alistair didn't know what he was doing. He just felt this

DAVID BEERS & MICHAEL ANDERLE

was right. Something in him said this wasn't a dim-witted beast that only knew reproduction and hunger. Something said it was closer to a drathe than a wolf.

"I'm sorry," Alistair called across the space separating them. "I didn't know. I didn't understand."

The creature screamed, baring its teeth. It rose on its back legs, and its talons slashed the air hard enough for a *whoosh* to whistle past him.

He holstered his Whip. "I'm sorry. I didn't know what I was doing. I do now. I understand." He lifted his left hand slowly, then pointed at the circle. "We will all die now for my stupidity unless you forgive me. It's up to you."

Then Alistair did something idiotic. He turned his back on the beast.

The roc's front talons hit the ground. The animal didn't shriek. It didn't rush its enemy. It dropped its beak and took a deep breath. Dust swirled around the steel-colored beak. It stared at the man, the eyes showing a deep-seated intelligence. Something foreign, yes, but something akin as well.

Alistair looked to his right and found Caesar. The giant was nodding as if he knew something. Nero stood next to him, and that maniacal grin was on his face.

Alistair wasn't sure if he was going to die at this moment. If it was to be so, he would accept it. He didn't want to kill that creature, or the others around him. They'd been kidnapped from their homes and ridden here for a battle. Let them go back home. Let them live their lives. His quarrel was elsewhere.

Alistair heard the massive flap of wings and felt the rush of wind. He didn't know if it was coming for him or something else, but he closed his eyes and turned his face to the ground. He hoped for a warrior's death if that was what was necessary.

The scream came from higher than Alistair had expected, then he heard the flap of more wings as the remaining rocs pulled into the sky after their leader. Alistair opened his eyes and tilted his head upward.

They were leaving—every last one of them.

Caesar walked across the expanse as the other gigantes knelt once again, their heads bowed. Nero remained standing, still smiling, although he didn't approach Alistair.

The giant walked in front of Alistair and lightly placed his hand over the wound. Alistair met the gigante's eyes and felt the nanotech find the wound and begin healing it. Caesar grimaced for a second, then his face relaxed.

"Did you know?" Alistair asked.

Caesar nodded.

"Why didn't you tell me what they were?"

Caesar didn't respond but only stared at him, and Alistair thought he understood. Even now, he wasn't sure he could describe the creature he'd just encountered. Made by man, they might have surpassed that which the gods had made. Caesar might not have had the words to describe them either.

"I had to see it for myself, didn't I?" Alistair asked.

"A true leader must know how to humble himself." Caesar pulled his huge hand from Alistair's side. He gave a small nod, then walked back to the circle of gigantes. He knelt like those around him and bowed his head.

Thoreaux ran to the middle of the muddy field. "What

in Hades was all that about?" Thoreaux asked. "I thought we were all dead."

"Me too." He glanced past Thoreaux at the kneeling Caesar. Only Nero remained standing. "I don't have to kill everyone to beat the Commonwealth. I just need to kill those who deserve it, and whatever they are, they didn't deserve it."

Thoreaux watched the rocs flying in the distance. One of them at the back was slower than the rest. It carried the dead animal in its talons. "Maybe you're right. Either way, what do we do next? From the looks of things, you've added to your army."

Alistair stood and slowly turned to see all those kneeling. "We do what we came here for. We set them and all the rest free."

THE WRITTEN HISTORY OF THE GREAT INSURRECTION

There are those across the universe who say Alistair Kane —Prometheus—is a ruthless murderer. His mythology has grown so far and wide that many think of him as a reborn god. Some say he is the entire universe's reckoning, while others claim he will send mankind back to the Dark Ages with his reckless crusade.

I watched him on that planet, the one where he went to free the gigantes. Legends have spread, all of them false. No bird creatures lifted him on their wings and carried him to victory. No gigantes welcomed him with open arms. He didn't speak to fish or walk on water.

He went there and nearly died multiple times. He is modified, true, but he is still human. He was fallible, and in the end, he had humanity's frailties as well. He got lost in the need to conquer at all costs, or he nearly did. For a long time, Alistair Kane had been a tool that broke others. Anything that stood up to him fell beneath the sheer force of his will and body.

It was there that he changed. He became more than the

tool of destruction. He became more than the Commonwealth or the missile seeking to blow it up.

He, perhaps for the first time in his life, became something more than human. Something greater than a warrior.

The legend that people should talk about is how he offered peace and an apology. Perhaps that is the true measure of a man. Looking back on everything we've done, I may be proudest of him at that moment.

CHAPTER NINETEEN

Servia had almost given up hope for the man who had left the ship two weeks ago. The first four days or so had been as stressful as any she could remember. No one knew whether those below were still alive. There'd been no more messages from the corporation, and when they looked down on the jungle, they saw nothing from their high vantage point.

They'd seen the flames burn the vast area, and everyone had hoped that hadn't been the end of the loved ones they'd sent down there. They couldn't know though, not for sure. Not yet. The AllMother said she couldn't see anything. She was too far away and the planet was too large for her to find them. For the first time in a long time, though, she gave her opinion.

"Trust him. I still do."

It wasn't until five or six days later—Servia wasn't sure —that they saw the first signs of Pro's work.

Servia had held it together over those first days, doing her best to keep a stiff upper lip.

When she saw the fires, she knew they were from Prometheus. There were so many of them dotting the landscape that they couldn't possibly be anything else. They stretched on for miles.

The first person she'd called to view them with her was Faitrin. The woman wept as she looked through the darkness at the hundreds, perhaps thousands, of fires that Pro's troops were making at night to cook their food and keep warm.

Servia called the rest of his council to her. "Look," she said and pointed at the holovid in front of her.

Relm's eyes widened, and the AllMother gave a small smile.

"He's doing it," she said.

Servia broadcasted that holovid to the entire dreadnought. A roar went up from the gigantes when they saw the night fires. They more than anyone knew what it meant. The liberation of their kind.

When the room had cleared, Servia allowed herself to weep. She knew it wasn't over. Prometheus had still not contacted them, and although the fires moved closer to the city, more showing up with each passing night, they still hadn't reached it.

Still, she felt relief.

For now, they lived.

Maybe not forever, but for now.

Ave, Prometheus, Servia thought.

There simply wasn't any other way to get to the main corporation. They had no method of flight, and Alistair certainly wouldn't try to wrangle any rocs. No, it was by foot that they would reach their enemies.

In truth, it was the best way. It took longer, but Alistair came to understand his army in a way he never could have with quicker movement. He commanded they move through all of the games, from sector to sector, and as they ventured farther from the original, his fame grew.

The word spread.

You could fight if you wanted, but you would lose. So many gigantes were already following him, no individual clan could hope to overcome him. More, by joining, you would have the chance to march on the makers. That was where Prometheus the Fire Bringer was heading.

Alistair let the legends grow across the planet as day after day passed. It wasn't anything he was comfortable with, but he understood the necessity. The legend bred compliance, and the end goal was what mattered. Freeing the gigantes. Giving them choices. Stopping the insane breeding that took place here.

Alistair understood why the powers that be hadn't simply burned them alive, or he figured he did. He thought the corporation was too frightened to burn their entire inventory. From the scouts Alistair sent ahead, the corporation also believed they could stop Alistair's advance when he reached their city.

That was their plan: kill him when he arrived at their gates and simultaneously save their inventory.

Maybe they would, but Alistair was going all the same.

Night fell once again, and the fires burned for long

miles. Alistair stood on a hill and looked down at them, each one a symbol. They believed in him, just as the AllMother's troops had in the beginning. Each fire symbolized that belief.

He heard Thoreaux approaching behind him.

"What do the scouts say?" he asked.

"It's a formidable defense, Pro. They've got a lot of those droids we saw when we landed here. Hundreds. They're going to be hard to bring down, and they've got air support." Thoreaux was quiet for a moment, then asked, "Are you sure this is what we want to do? A lot of gigantes are going to die tomorrow if we go through with it."

Alistair put both hands on his hips. "They're going to die if we don't do it and in much the same fashion, except it will be at the behest of and for the monetary gain of someone else. Tomorrow, many may die, but the ones who survive will never have to fight or die for anyone else again."

Thoreaux said nothing, only stared at the campfires.

"How is Caesar?" Alistair asked after a few minutes of silence.

"Quiet. He hasn't said much to me or anyone else."

"Nero?"

"He might be the only gigante talking. I can't be certain, but he might be drunk. He sounds half-crazy either way."

Alistair understood it. To many of the gigantes, they were going up against their gods tomorrow: the makers, those who gave them life. Whether or not they were evil, they were still life-givers. Perhaps some of the gigantes thought they couldn't win. Alistair couldn't know the end of any battle, but he'd come through hell to get here, starting with jumping from that building when the Titans chased him. Perhaps they would lose, or maybe fate was at their back, propelling them forward. Alistair didn't care either way. He'd made up his mind that those who pitted gigante against gigante would see him at dawn tomorrow.

"Have as many as you can gather at this hill two hours before dawn. I'd like to address as many as I can."

"Yes, sir," Thoreaux said. He stood in silence for a few more moments, then clapped his hand on Alistair's back.

Alistair thought back to what Faitrin had said: the change in Thoreaux, the added ruthlessness. He hoped it would be here tomorrow. They were going to need it.

The masses stood before Alistair. He wondered if this was what ancient Roman generals had felt like before battle. He'd never addressed such a huge crowd of warriors, and he wondered if anyone alive had. Most of the human race had not done serious battle for centuries, certainly nothing like what was to come tomorrow.

Thousands of soldiers were spread before him. They were nearly two miles from the city's outskirts. When he was finished addressing them, they would begin their descent on the makers.

Alistair had placed his helmet on, pulling back the face-plate so they could see him as he spoke. The armor would still amplify his voice a great deal. Most below him would be able to hear him.

"Many of you only know me by name. Only some have seen me up close. Even fewer have seen me in battle."

He started pacing to his right, looking down at the ground as he spoke.

"Most of you have only heard of me. Prometheus. The Fire Bringer. The Roc-Killer. The Liberator." He stopped walking and looked at the warriors. "I don't care what you call me so long as you understand my purpose. I came here for one reason." He turned slightly and pointed toward the city. "To go there and kill those who enslave you."

He looked down at his feet and basked in the silence.

"You and I are very similar, although you may not think so. Some of you may have heard why I fight. The truth is, I'm fighting my gods, *my makers*, too. First they enslaved me without my knowing it, just as you all have been, then they tried to kill me. I refused, and now I rise against them. In a very short time, you will all get the chance to tell those who wish to hold power over you that they have no right."

Again, he looked at the giants.

"You will have the chance to tell them that you would rather *die* than let them hold that power. I cannot guarantee victory, but I can promise you this. I will die by your side rather than let them rule you."

He held his hand out and Thoreaux stepped up, giving him a blade.

"Where I come from, and what I was, we have a ritual that we do every time we go into battle." He retracted the armor on his right wrist, revealing the still-scabbing wound from his last battle. "I will do it now, and if you wish to partake, I invite you. You only need to repeat after me, and in the end, draw your own blood."

Alistair knelt, the blade in his left hand. His face was still scabbed with the cuts from his fight with the roc. He knew he looked hellish, like a warrior born in Hades. What was one more cut?

He said the words, his voice echoing to the mass of killers.

And he heard the words coming back to him, thousands performing the ritual that only an elite few had been gifted to know on Earth.

"See it and fear," his voice echoed down the hill. "See it and die."

Alistair drew his blood, then he smeared it across his cut-up face.

He looked up. Eager giant heads stared at him, blood dripping down their cheeks like monsters born from nightmares.

Caesar stepped up to his left. His shout echoed down the hill. "*Ave*, Prometheus!"

The valley filled with the shouts.

Ave.

Prometheus.

CHAPTER TWENTY

The planet's star rose on the horizon as the opposing armies approached. The sounds of thousands of gigante footfalls echoed off massive buildings that stretched to the sky.

Alistair was gone, no longer needed. Prometheus had stepped forward, ready to do what was necessary.

He walked with Thoreaux on his right and Caesar on his left.

Pro stared forward, seeing the end of their travels and the tower he'd dreamed of. It looked the same as it had in his dream, only now the glass windows glittered from the birthing sun instead of being shattered. He didn't know how many would die here, but he knew the three of them would end up in that tower.

He knew that the chance of death for all three of them was very real.

Pro hadn't said a word to anyone about this. He just marched forward.

The quadcopters came for them first.

It was only later that Thoreaux would be able to piece together what he'd witnessed. While he was in the battle, he saw very little he understood outside of what came into his immediate purview. Everything that showed up *there* died. He supposed he'd been lucky no one he knew showed up in front of him because Thoreaux felt certain he would have cut them down as well.

Something took him over that he didn't fully understand, but he embraced it all the same.

For the first time in his life, Thoreaux felt free.

In other times, that mindset had been known as "bloodlust." Thoreaux saw it as freedom.

Blood drenched him, and still he pushed forward. He knew where they were heading. Pro had told them all.

The tallest tower in the middle. That was their objective, and Thoreaux was leaving a trail of bodies behind as he made his way there.

Everything ceased to matter besides those two things—getting to the tower and killing everything on his way.

Prometheus no longer mattered. The AllMother and her entire Insurrection didn't matter. Even Faitrin didn't matter.

Killing those who opposed him had turned into a god, and Thoreaux worshipped at its feet.

Prometheus finally came to a halt.

For the past hour, he had felt like he'd been in perpetual motion. He'd fought relentlessly, at some points confident of making it to the tower, and other times thinking everything would crumble. Pro had kept an eye on Thoreaux, having to rescue him more than once in their push forward. He didn't think Thoreaux even noticed, not where he was in relation to his allies or that Prometheus had bailed him out.

He'd continually pushed too deep into enemy territory, surrounding himself with droids and gigantes who fought for the other side. They were about to overwhelm him each time when Prometheus showed up, giving him the support he needed.

Now Prometheus stood at the base of the tower. He turned and looked at the wake of destruction his army had left.

Fire littered the battlefield. He could see the wreckage of at least four quadcopters. The death those things had created was sickening, and it had taken entirely too long to bring them all down. However, they were finished, and Prometheus still breathed.

The battle was nearly over. There were small groups still skirmishing, but the gigantes who followed Prometheus were overwhelming the remaining forces.

Thoreau approached with his eyes on the tower. "*Ave,* Prometheus," he whispered as he arrived.

Caesar and Nero were coming now, their core group having survived this battle when many others lay dead or dying. The gigante had used their nanotech to save and heal as many as they could, but in the end, death came all the same.

What does that mean, Allie? That so many others died while those you need the most remain on their feet?

Prometheus didn't know, and he didn't have time to care now. The two gigantes approached as he turned to stare at the tower. This was something he'd done a lot in his previous life—assaults on tall buildings. It might be the thing he had perfected in his life, yet he knew what was about to happen.

He'd seen it.

The giant standing above Caesar, ready to deliver a killing blow. A man wearing a suit holding a weapon on Thoreaux. A quadcopter coming for all of them.

"Caesar, Thoreaux, remember my dream," he said from behind his faceplate as he lowered his head to look at the door.

"In case you want to walk away. I'm going up, but that doesn't mean any of you have to."

Thoreaux raised both eyebrows as he turned to look at the door. "Well, Pro, if your dreams tell the truth, I don't think we have a choice in the matter. If you've seen us up there, we're going to go up there, right?"

"I don't know," he answered honestly. "I just wanted to remind you about what I've seen."

"Yeah, if I die up there, I'll blame my stupid decision to follow you on fate, thus absolving me of any responsibility for said decision." He grinned. "I'm pretty sure I can speak for the giant standing next to you. If you're going in, we're going in."

Caesar nodded. "Little man speaks for me."

Nero was on the far left, standing next to Caesar. "I will not go. Death is in that place for me, and there is no chance of stopping it. No one but you three should enter. Anyone else who tries will never make it to that top floor."

Pro nodded. "You're right. I want you to make sure no one else enters the building. We'll see you when we get back down."

Nero was looking at the building as if it held some sort of magic. Perhaps for him, it did. Or maybe he was seeing something no one else could. He turned and stuck his arm out, the same as Alistair had done that first battle morning. "It has been an honor. I hope to see you again."

Prometheus stood and gripped the gigante's arm. "It's been an honor for me too. I'll see you when we get back." He meant both things. What Caesar had said in the beginning no longer held any weight for Alistair. They would not kill this gigante. He was their friend now, and Prometheus planned to bring everyone back.

He could see in Nero's eyes that the gigante wasn't sure any of them would live through this episode. The dream had said the same thing.

But people had been saying that to Prometheus since this started. Ares. The Commonwealth. Everyone else who'd gotten in his way.

The person upstairs who'd created this horror story of a planet would soon find out what the rest had.

Prometheus was a war machine. One who created his own rules for the games put before him.

He turned back to the building. There was nothing else to be said out here or in there. His Whip was still unfurled, and its communication would involve no words. Pro went forward, his two lieutenants quickly following him. They reached the double door, which was made of opaque glass, and it opened for them as if welcoming them inside.

Prometheus had just destroyed an army, but maybe those in here knew something he didn't.

His group entered the welcome area, and the double doors slid closed behind him.

A single man stood on the other side of the welcome area. Prometheus' HUD zeroed in on him and showed that he was much, much older and held no weapons.

"Hello!" he called. "I have no weapons and mean none of you any harm! My voice hasn't been used in quite some time, so if you'll come a bit closer, I'd very much appreciate it!"

Pro and Thoreaux scanned the room at the same time. His HUD registered no weapons. The room seemed safe, but out of everything that could have been in here, this wasn't even imaginable. "We all need to be ready for anything. Whatever that man over there looks like, it's deception. We might end up dead in the next few minutes, no matter how cheery he sounds."

Thoreaux started forward. His armor was coated in older dried blood plus a newer splash. It rolled off him in fat drops, splashing on the floor and creating a trail as he made his way to the strange old man. They stopped a few feet from him. This wasn't the man from Pro's dream. He would be in the end room. "Do you know why I'm here?"

"I have been asleep for a long time," the old man said. "Longer than any of you might be capable of imagining, and let's just say my offspring isn't as capable as I would have liked. Otherwise, you two gentlemen and this gigante would not be standing here right now. My son, the poor child, actually believes you are a god come down from the universe to wreak havoc on this planet. I'm going to assume that isn't true, correct?"

Prometheus was listening to the man's words but also letting his senses give him everything else that was happening around him. He knew it mattered nothing what this man said. He was a threat, perhaps the greatest one Prometheus had ever faced. "You are correct. I'm flesh and blood."

The old man chuckled and looked at the floor. He shook his head. "You try to teach your children about the gods, then they go getting superstitious when the first real warrior shows up. I suppose it is my fault, but that is neither here nor there. You asked me a question. Do I know what you're here for? I think I do from all the dead outside, plus what remains of my inventory beginning to stand in rows behind you. You want all of them for yourself, but rather than purchase them, you'd just kill everyone and leave? That about right?"

Prometheus looked at the floor, momentarily forgetting his surroundings in the exasperation he felt. "Your kind are all the same. You cannot think of a universe where someone doesn't want to accumulate more power." He looked back up. "I'm here to free them and make sure no more are created in the way you've done."

The old man smiled. He looked like he could be someone's kindly grandfather. "No such universe exists, my good man. Own them or free them, in the end, you want them to follow you. To do your bidding. To help you achieve whatever war it is that you're fighting. It doesn't concern me, to be honest. Your wants and mine are in opposition. That is all that matters, but it would seem I've been bested in a way I never thought possible. I planned for a lot of things, but an invasion by one warlord?" He waved away the suggestion. "It was so improbable as to be virtually impossible."

"And yet, here I am," Prometheus responded.

The old man's smile widened. "Here you are. I can see when I've been bested. There is no need for any more violence. I find it horrific. If you want control of the empire, come upstairs to my son's office, and I will sign it over to you. I don't know if the document will hold up in the intergalactic courts, given that you've destroyed my capital city. Then again, intergalactic courts don't hold much sway, so I think you should be fine."

"Whatever you say," Prometheus responded. "I'm ready for this to end."

The old man dropped his smile and gave a slight nod of acknowledgment. "Then let's end it." He stepped to the side and gestured at an opening elevator. "Shall we?"

Prometheus didn't look at the old man as he passed. He didn't consider the illogic of issues with knowing the future or whether he could just walk away and change it. His will, harder than steel, controlled this situation. He wanted to free these creatures, and the only way to do it was by getting to that last room.

He stepped into the elevator. Thoreaux got in to his right, Caesar to his left. The old man stepped on last, turning his back to the three of them as if this was just a simple business venture. The doors shut, and the elevator began rising automatically. The old man was silent.

Prometheus turned his head to the right and left, finding the other two staring at the man, ready to kill him if need be.

For Thoreaux, perhaps need was not a motivator.

The elevator continued its rise for over a minute, going higher and higher into the building.

It finally came to a slow stop on the top floor, a bell ringing from above. The doors opened, and the old man stepped out onto the floor. Prometheus followed with his Whip unfurled. Thoreaux and Caesar were one step behind him.

Pro scanned from left to right. The floor appeared to be a single office, although there were different rooms throughout it. To the right, an open doorway showed a dining room. The door to the right was closed, and before him was an office-looking office. A desk sat in the middle of the room, with a single chair behind it and none in front. There were holovid screens to the left and right of it.

Prometheus' eyes landed on the only other person in the room, a thin younger man who stood to the right of the desk. Pro recognized the face immediately. It was the man who would hold a weapon on Thoreaux very shortly. There was more to see here, though, and Prometheus reined in his desire to leap across the room and cut the man down.

"My son," the old man said with a gesture as he moved to the desk.

Prometheus dialed back the speaker on his helmet. "That's one of them."

The other two didn't respond.

The old man made his way to the desk and sat down in

the chair. He pulled a small pile of papers from the left side of the desk to the center. "My son here will sign as a witness. I will sign as controller of the corporation, and you as the purchaser. Before you leave, I will give you a transit number to put the requested credit in. It is a small sum that you should easily be able to afford, but some number is necessary for the courts. It's for your protection." He looked up from the papers, and his face showed no mirth or grandfatherly friendliness. The man in front of Prometheus was a straight-up killer.

Pro lowered his Whip to the ground and it burnt the marble floor. He started walking, dragging the Whip behind him and creating three deep black trails. He stopped in front of the desk and left the Whip burning through the floor. "Are you ready to stop the charade?"

The old man leaned back in his chair and folded his arms over one another. "Yes. I suppose I am."

Prometheus raised the Whip as quickly as a viper lunges, but it was still too slow.

It must have been the chair leaning back that triggered the explosion.

The walls behind Prometheus burst forward with more force than his suit could handle. It wasn't fire but wind. Pro's mind saw everything even though his body couldn't react. A field of some sort rushed up from the floor, covering both the old man and the son. The glass walls on the exterior of the building exploded outward as the torrent of wind rushed forward. Prometheus rose into the air, hands and Whip forward. The desk went forward too, breaking on the shield that surrounded the old man.

Prometheus rushed past him too quickly to even attempt grabbing him.

After that, there was nothing to see but the outside city because Prometheus was thrown from the building's top floor and began his descent.

CHAPTER TWENTY-ONE

Thoreaux rose off the ground, his mind able to keep up at the same pace as his leader's. All he knew was that he was flying forward, something had exploded behind him, and he was going to die in the next few moments when he flew out of the shattered windows.

He slammed into something unseen, his left arm and armor taking the brunt of the impact. He felt his bones snap all the way up to his shoulder and he remained pinned against the unseen forcefield, the wind behind him continuing to rush.

"Enough."

The old man's voice boomed across the room, and the torrential wind stopped. Thoreaux hit the floor, excruciating pain filling his torso and a burning need to kill filling his mind.

His right arm pushed him up, and he looked forward. The younger man was standing in front of him, holding a weapon that looked similar to a MechPulse in his hands.

He took two steps forward, and Thoreaux had no doubt that the piece would kill him even with his armor on.

He looked to his right. Prometheus was gone, and a giant unlike anything Thoreaux had ever seen was kicking Caesar's head and ribs. His friend was on his side, trying to curl up and unable to defend himself. The giant had come from the far-right door. The blows rained down as if a god were delivering them.

The old man stood up. Thoreaux didn't know how the two of them had survived the explosion, but it didn't matter much at that moment.

"I'd sooner destroy the entire universe than give up my company," the old man said. He didn't look at Thoreaux or Caesar as he moved to the unharmed elevator. The doors opened, and he stepped inside. "Finish this," he told his son.

The doors shut behind Thoreaux.

The young man kept the gun leveled at Thoreaux's head. "Take your helmet off."

Thoreaux slowly got up on his knees. Using his right hand, he removed the helmet and let it drop to the floor. The blows to Caesar continued; the giant who was delivering them didn't seem to know anyone else was in the room.

The young man holding the weapon glanced quickly over his shoulder. Had Thoreaux not shattered everything from his pinky to his collarbone, he would have been able to get control of the situation. As it was, the glance behind him was done with far too quickly, and Thoreaux was in the same position as before. "Looks like Dad was right. He wasn't a god. He got the lucky draw here. We're about to make an example out of you two."

Thoreaux needed to hear nothing else. He'd die on this floor before any more torture happened.

He lunged forward, the Fire Starter armor amplifying his speed.

The young man fired.

Prometheus fell.

The world sped past him quicker than even he could keep up with.

His heart rate was still one hundred beats per minute. His mind remained focused, not panicked. He understood two things. He had to stop his fall, and he had to get back up to that top floor.

He was falling with his stomach facing the ground. He knew what he had to do and also that it might rip his body apart when he did it.

There wasn't any choice, and there wasn't any time.

Pro altered his leg position slightly. His body straightened and turned so he was facing the building. The glass whipped past him as he rushed to the ground. He tried to time it right, knowing if he missed, both arms would be ripped off his body.

He stretched his hands forward, fingers out. The glass in front of him shattered, but he'd hit it right. He continued his fall for another second, then his hands were grappling the floor. He wasn't strong enough to stop himself, so the fall continued to another floor, but he'd managed to slow himself enough to stop on *that* one.

He hung in the air, his Fire Starter suit doing the heavy

lifting in keeping him from dying. He glanced below and quickly turned his head back up.

"Yeah, no need to do that again," he whispered to himself.

He had two options now. He could pull himself onto this floor and hope he could fight his way through whatever was waiting for him. Or...

He could leapfrog up the building and attack in the least expected way.

It wasn't a hard choice.

Using every bit of his strength, Pro pulled with his arms and got his legs up to the floor. He pushed off, and to those on the ground, he might have looked like he was flying. His body propelled itself up two floors at a time, where he found purchase again, then rose once more.

Yes, to those on the ground, it must have been a strange and wondrous sight to see, a man taking flight.

Prometheus ascended the building in mere seconds.

He reached the top floor and hopped inside, unfurling his Whip in the same movement.

Things weren't the same as they'd been in his dream, but they were very similar, if worse. Caesar wasn't on his knees but the floor, and a gigante had paused mid-kick to look at Pro.

Thoreaux lay on his stomach, his eyes open, blood leaking from his mouth. The young man from earlier held a weapon to his head and was staring with wide eyes. The color was gone from his face. "He's not dead yet, but he will be if you take another step."

The gigante pulled two blades from his back and put them both against Caesar's head.

Here was the choice. One could live. He would have to choose. Pro didn't hear the quadcopter, but that didn't matter anymore.

The decision was his.

Thoreaux or Caesar.

"No," he whispered.

"Wh-wh-what?" the man stuttered.

Prometheus wasn't talking to him. He was speaking to the situation. He knew what he was going to do, but he didn't know if it would be possible. The sheer concentration was going to be harder than anything he'd ever attempted, let alone accomplished.

It was the only non-choice because Prometheus knew he couldn't choose. They would both die or neither of them.

He closed his eyes, and that black space returned. Two white shapes formed in it, the gigante over Caesar and the man holding the weapon. His mind moved forward, zooming in on the shapes. The chest. The trigger.

He could barely hold both in his mind because he had to do two different things with them at the same time.

"*GET ON THE FUCKING FLOOR!*" the man shouted, his voice cracking through the black space in his mind.

"No," Prometheus whispered.

His body stretched forward, his right leg going down in a lunge as his right hand flung the Whip at the gigante's chest. He remained in that position, his arm outstretched in a follow-through, his body rigid in its lunge.

The Whip plunged into the giant's chest, sinking through his arm and bone. The force of the throw shoved the giant toward the door he'd come through. Blood erupted from his mouth. He kept standing, although his hands were shaking, and he'd dropped the blades.

Prometheus didn't open his eyes as he slowly stood, turning to face the young man.

"*WHAT THE FUCK ARE YOU DOING?*" the man screamed, his voice as high as a child's.

Prometheus' focus was total. The man's trigger finger couldn't move. Pro crossed the office in a step and knocked the weapon from his hand. It clattered to the floor, and he grabbed the man by his hair and dragged him over to Caesar. The man cried out, but Pro ignored it. He knelt in front of Caesar, using his other free hand to turn the giant's face up.

Caesar's eyes were open and looking at him.

"Thoreaux needs you, okay? I have more to do."

Caesar nodded. Pro knew the pain the big creature was in, and he knew from the blood leaking out of Thoreaux's mouth that he was dying. He also knew his job wasn't finished.

He pulled Caesar to his feet. The giant groaned and gripped his ribs with both arms.

Pro pointed at Thoreaux. "Hurry."

The nanotech was already pouring out of the gigante's hands, flooding toward his second in command. It was more than Pro had ever seen come from the giant, and he understood the personal toll it would take on him.

If it didn't save Thoreaux, nothing could.

"Come on," Prometheus growled at the man hanging from his fist by his hair.

The other giant was on his knees, still bleeding from his mouth but still not falling over. Pro grabbed the Whip's hilt and pulled up instead of out, slicing up the gigante's chest and through his collarbone.

Weapon and soon-to-be-dead man in hand, he went to the elevator. The doors opened for him, and he stepped on. "Take me to your father. Say anything other than where to go, and I'll remove a piece of your body. The Whip will cauterize it, so you don't have to worry about bleeding out. Trust me when I say I'm a surgeon with this and can take a lot of pieces off you before I kill you."

"Buh-buh-basement," the man sputtered.

Pro touched the button, and the elevator started descending. He imagined that the elevator was reading the son's biometrics, and that was why it worked. He also imagined that the man in the basement thought his son was coming to tell him it was finished.

Prometheus had learned a very important lesson on this planet. Arrogance kills.

"Why did he keep the other two alive?" Prometheus asked without looking down at his crying captive.

"To make an example out of them."

Pro understood. More arrogance. The old man figured he was too dangerous, so he'd kill him right off the bat, then he would torture his followers to teach any other wannabe heroes what happened to those who messed with the company. The arrogance was thinking he didn't need to ensure that Pro was dead. That he didn't even need to remain in the room until everything was finished. What he said should happen would just happen.

Now the old man would learn a lesson, too.

Finish the fucking job.

The elevator opened, and Prometheus walked into a

room that looked nothing like a basement. There was some kind of tube on the left side that was open, wires running in and out of it. The old man was at a desk with a metal cap on, wires coming off it as well. A droid stood at his side, looking like it was taking measurements of the hat.

The old man didn't look up from the DataTrack on his table. "Is it done?"

"Almost." Pro stepped to the table, raised his Whip, and decapitated the old man.

He didn't look at the droid as he cut it half, then brought the Whip down to the man on his knees. He shoved it into his chest, hearing the muffled scream.

Pro released the young man's head, and he collapsed on the floor. He stepped to the other side of the desk. The head was on the floor, the man's eyes still blinking. The body remained sitting in the chair. Prometheus shoved it to the floor and sat down. He discarded the helmet, dropping it on the floor as well.

He pulled the DataTrack to him. It was still open, all the communication tools available to him. It didn't take long for him to shut down the communication block with the dreadnought.

"Come get us," he said into the DataTrack, sending a tracking position with the message.

He put his head on the table and closed his eyes. The warrior slid back and the man came forth. Exhaustion wasn't even a tenth of what he felt. He was drained down to his soul. How many had he killed today? How many more would he need to kill? Would Thoreaux survive?

Could he keep going? Could he see this through?

It was Luna's face that came to him. Her beauty shone in the blackness of his mind's eye.

I love you, he thought. *All of this is for you.*

With the dead surrounding him, Alistair wondered if he was selling his soul for her.

He wondered if he'd already done it.

THE WRITTEN HISTORY OF THE GREAT INSURRECTION

We took over a planet. There was a lot left to do after the war was finished. There was the board left to deal with, the laboratories, the scientists, the entire economy created and sustained by the subjugation of a species.

All of that would come in time. We would see to it.

With each great feat Prometheus achieved, more eyes fell on him.

This sacking of a planet was no different.

Distant ears, ones we didn't know about, were hearing his name now.

Hearing *Ave,* Prometheus...and wondering if they might be next in this warrior's quest to find his wife.

Many of the beings now looking at Prometheus wouldn't wait to find out.

They'd come see about him first.

The story continues with Prometheus Unites available at Amazon and through Kindle Unlimited.

Claim your copy today!

Even after writing a lot of books, there's still a sense of amazement that someone actually *reads* them. I don't think I'll ever lose that awe; so, thank you – you made my day.

Alistair learned a lot in this book, but he still has more lessons ahead of him. A lot of my own life goes into my novels, and I think I'm at a stage in my life where I'm having to learn some pretty important things. Sometimes the lessons are easy, but sometimes I make them hard, and it perhaps feels a bit like a giant bird-creature trying to decapitate you.

The lessons don't get easier for Alistair, I promise, but if he can master them, he'll find they're rewarding.

Perhaps that's true for all of us.

Prometheus Unites is next.

Come with me, and let's see what awaits. Can Alistair keep learning in order to once again be with his wife? Or are the lessons going to grow too hard?

-db

AUTHOR NOTES - MICHAEL ANDERLE
WRITTEN JULY 7, 2021

Thank you for both reading this book and these author notes in the back.

This book, I'm going to speak about one of the challenging aspects of running a publishing company such as LMBPN.

It's not rocket science, but it is starting to feel like it.

What am I talking about? *Covers.*

So, LMBPN puts out between 320-400 new covers a year. Some of these covers are for our new series (the problem children are the book ones of the series.) Some of the covers are for the multi-box sets where we need a special image created that (often) uses the first book in the series plus the other covers as spinal images.

But not always because that would be too easy.

Other covers are required when we are re-branding existing series (such as *The Kurtherian Gambit* books 01-21 are in production to recover all of them.) We are also in the middle of a recover for the twenty-two books in *The Unbelievable Mr. Brownstone.*

267

Just between those two series, we will need over forty new covers.

We are proud that our covers ROCK, or we try to make them do so. We don't always hit the mark with some of the series, so then we go back and give them a new coat of paint.

For others, we know that they will be good for years (such as the *Skharr DeathEater* covers.) Fortunately, one doesn't recover Sword & Sorcery stories very often. This is good, those painting-style covers are e.x.p.e.n.s.i.v.e.

The covers for this series are pretty on point, but it took a little while to dial in what the effort would look and how we imagined a whole table full of these books might look.

To feed the art-monster (covers, social images, advertising images, etc.) LMBPN sources four to five artists and asks for all the time that they can provide us.

It's a lot.

Sometimes—meaning every couple of weeks—we realize that someone (not pointing any fingers at myself) has gummed up the works by placing a new series on the production schedule while failing to let cover production know we need art.

Fast forward a few weeks to audio catalog preparation and we realize we have no scheduled book cover for something that needs to be done...usually in two weeks and you can hear "MIKE!" screamed from one state here in America to another.

I try like hell to be busy writing something—anything—and keep my head buried when those mistakes occur.

The reason this is top of mind is I just got off an

unscheduled conference call that roped in an author, an artist, and the lady responsible for keeping the schedule clean and the artists sane.

And me.

Generally, I'm the one who caused the problem.

(The issue was actually a scheduling problem that was exacerbated by a COVID situation. Not me...*this time.*)

Obviously, having to schedule a few hundred covers while everything is in a state of flux is not as difficult as rocket science.

It just feels like it. For about an hour, then we leave thinking we have it in the bag.

Until you hear a small voice coming over the winds from the East...

"MIIIIIKKKKEEE!"

Ad Aeternitatem,

Michael Anderle

Nemesis

She's coming and no one can stop her...

An alien Queen, Morena, was removed from power and forced into exile. Doomed to roam space forever, with no hope of return.

Until a random party brings a man named Michael to her crashed ship. For the first time in millennia, Morena sees her salvation. First, in Michael ... and then Earth. The perfect place to repopulate her species. And those already here? **They can bow or die.**

As Morena begins her conquest, can Michael warn the world before it's too late? Can anyone stop the most powerful force the world has ever seen?

Earth's final Nemesis has arrived.

Don't miss this pulse-pounding science fiction series! If you love thought provoking thrill-rides, grab this book today!

The Singularity

One thousand years in the future, humans no longer rule...

In the early twenty-first century, humanity marveled at its greatest creation: Artificial Intelligence. They never foresaw the consequences of such a creation, though...

Now, in a world where humans must meet specifications to continue living, a man named Caesar emerges. Different, both in thought and talent, Caesar somehow slipped through the genetic net meant to catch those like him.

Eyes are falling on Caesar now, though, and he can no longer hide. The Artificial Intelligence wants him dead, but others want him to lead their revolution...

Can one man stand against humanity's greatest creation? A don't-miss epic science fiction novel that pits one man fighting for the future of all people!

Red Rain

What would you do if you couldn't stop killing?

John Hilt lives The American Dream. His corner office looks out on Dallas's beautiful skyline. His amazing wife and children love him. His father and sister adore him. John has it all.

Except every few years, when Harry shows back up. Harry wants John to kill people. Harry wants to watch the world burn.

Murderous thoughts take hold of John, and as flames ignite across his life, the sky doesn't send cool rain water, but blood to feed their hunger.

If you love taut, psychological thrillers, grab Red Rain today and prepare to sleep with the lights on!

The Devil's Dream

He'll raise the dead, at all costs...

Perhaps the smartest man to ever live, Matthew Brand changed the world by twenty-five years old. In his mid-thirties, he still shaped the world as he wanted, until cops gunned down his son on the street.

Brand's life changed then. He forgot about bettering Earth and started trying to resurrect his son.

Eventually, Brand's mind overpowered even death's mysteries; he discovered how to bring back the dead--he only needed living bodies to make his son's life possible again. Why not use the bodies of those who killed his son? In the largest manhunt the FBI's ever experienced, how do they stop a man who can calculate all the odds and stack them in his favor?

CONNECT WITH THE AUTHORS

Connect with David and sign up for his email list here:

Email list
http://www.davidbeersauthor.com/mailing-list

Website
http://www.davidbeersfiction.com/

Social Media:

https://www.facebook.com/davidbeersauthor

Email List: http://lmbpn.com/email/

Connect with Michael and sign up for his email list here:

Website: http://lmbpn.com

Email List: http://lmbpn.com/email/

Social Media:

https://www.facebook.com/LMBPNPublishing

https://twitter.com/MichaelAnderle

https://www.instagram.com/lmbpn_publishing/

https://www.bookbub.com/authors/michael-anderle

www.ingramcontent.com/pod-product-compliance
Lightning Source LLC
Chambersburg PA
CBHW020402110726
47899CB00006B/1825